Messages from Nature

Messages from Nature

Patricia Daly-Lipe

2010

TABLE OF CONTENTS

ACKNOWLEDGEMENTS

It is beginning to dawn on (mankind) that the root of all good and evil lies in his own psyche and that the world around him is as he himself has shaped it; perhaps he dimly senses, too, that the fate of the world grows out of what happens in the psyches of human beings.

CARL JUNG

Universe to each must be
All that is, including me.
RICHARD BUCKMINSTER FULLER

The most powerful thoughts come from personal experience. The following short stories are true, significant and personal. Over the years, each story and/or poem was published in various magazines and newspapers: from Florida to Washington, DC, from Georgia to Virginia, from the Caribbean to California, as well as across the seas in England. Keeping the words of Jung and Buckminster Fuller in mind, please enjoy my experiences and acknowledge your own. Animals unhindered by human society's inhibitions and regulations and nature, adhering to its own rules and inclinations, can teach us, but only if we are willing to listen.

The act of writing is accomplished from within the creative confines of the author's soul. The act of editing is accomplished by those who can look at the writing and advise the best presentation for those writings. For the latter, I wish to thank Marni Lawson, an accomplished artist and a great friend, and that special man I am married to, retired physician, Steele Lipe, whose left-brained abilities are unsurpassed.

OTHER BOOKS BY PATRICIA DALY-LIPE

A CRUEL CALM, Paris Between the Wars
Myth, Magic and Metaphor, A Journey into the Heart of
Creativity
La Jolla, A Celebration of Its Past
ALL ALONE, Washington to Rome, A '60s Memoir

REVIEW OF THIS EDITION,
MESSAGES FROM NATURE

Patricia has done it again: mixed and matched brilliantly. The citations, the etymological meditations, the allusions to de Chardin's writing together with Steiner's reflections and Antoine E's magical writing are at the "heart" of things and an expression of moral courage in an immorally polluted world.

Joseph Roccasalvo, S.J.
Prof. of Comparative Religion and Buddhist Studies, Fordham University; Standing member of the Center for the Study of World religions, Harvard, where he earned his Ph.D.; Author of several books including *Portrait of a Woman*

REVIEWS OF FIRST EDITION KNOWN AS
NATURE'S WISDOM

Patricia Daly-Lipe has an incredible gift for writing about animals. Everything she writes is touching. Her deep love of animals is so clear and she has a talent for drawing the reader into the story.... I think she is amazing in that ability. I hope the world sees more animal-related literature from her.

Betsy Clark
USDF Gold Medalist

***

This is Patricia Daly-Lipe's gift: She tells your story—tells all of our stories—through her own experiences with beloved companions, animal and otherwise. The lean, wiry power of Daly-Lipe's wordcraft compels you to immerse yourself in her tales, knowing full well that her tales are your tales. It is a fast read, but don't be in a hurry; reign yourself in and savor the journey.

When you read *Nature's Wisdom*—and read it you must—you will, by turns, smile, laugh, cheer, weep, grieve, and heal. And most of all you will rejoice at the opportunity to be invited along the diverse paths of this talented writer's own journey in the unified company of empathy and compassion. The work chronicles Daly-Lipe's respect—and love—for all life.

When you experience, through Daly-Lipe, the abundant truths waiting Out There to be harvested by the diligent and willing among us, you will be in possession of glistening gems of nature's wisdom by their handfuls.

Patti Cole
Contributing Editor to *laJoie*
***

Nature's Wisdom is a delightful collection of personal stories about animals, people, travel, and the sea. The reader quickly sees that Patricia Daly Lipe is a special person who loves animals and thoroughly understands the special bond that only animals and humans can share.

It is also evident that she is an accomplished writer who loves travel and adventure. I particularly enjoyed her sailing recounts as I could almost feel the stillness of the too calm, quiet days and the fierceness of the stormy, windy days at sea.

In this complex world, it is particularly refreshing to find a writer who is able to help us stop, look, reflect, and learn invaluable life lessons that only Nature can teach us. I highly recommend this book.

Jane Best
Architect and photographic artist
North Carolina

***

Nature's Wisdom is an eclectic collection of short stories and poems, with the unusual twist of Daly-Lipe including some of her father's works at the end of this book….

Following the tried-and-tested recommendation to 'Write what you know about,' Daly-Lipe does exactly that, resulting in a patchwork quilt of light-hearted, easy-to-read autobiographical snap-shots of her travels in both the US and Europe, and the events in her life involving her pets.

And, Daly-Lipe suggests that, "If we listen, our animals will teach us more about love than most of our human friends can or will."

Then, the inclusion of Daly-Lipe's personal photos further adds to her carefully crafted words, as if any additions are needed!

This collection will particularly appeal to pet owners, animal lovers, nature lovers and travelers. I use the word "travelers" in both the context of physical and spiritual voyages alike. Indeed, Nature's Wisdom makes for a pleasant voyage on which to embark.

David Taub
Feature columnist for *Poetry Now*, Britain's largest circulating poetry and short-story magazine; Member of Britain's National Union of Journalists; Co-author of *Language of Souls*

***

Empowering with Love. This compact book is an enticing smorgasbord of Patricia Daly-Lipe's personal experiences with Nature, from her loving and psychic connections with animals to woman-empowerment by this svelte yet very competent, hardy sailor and impressive navigator of dangerous seas. Her Zen-like approach in this book of prose, also honorably including her father's works and other quotes, spellbound me. An inspiring book.

Tina Stonestreet
Medical Editor, Minister, Artist

SECTION I
Animal stories where the lesson is learned as the tale unfolds

Ethics is responsibility for all that lives extended until it knows no limits.
ALBERT SCHWEITZER

HOW DO WE MEASURE INTELLIGENCE?

Recently, I overheard someone comparing dogs to people. Their methodology of comparison used intelligence as the factor. My question then is how do you measure or define intelligence? Does compassion or empathy fit into this equation?

The other day, I heard a poignant tale. An older man was in the hospital and dying. His family received permission to have his companion dog allowed in the room for a last visit. The dog was ushered in and the door was closed. Fifteen minutes later, the family came back, opened the door expecting to escort the dog out. The patient was still in his bed. His arm was around his dog who had jumped onto the bed. The man was dead and his faithful dog had died beside him.

Empathy and compassion.

Sweet William was my wonderful, faithful companion. An English black and white cocker, he was my shadow. One day, I noticed his stool was white. I made an appointment with the vet but, at the last minute, was not able to take him. My daughter took William to the doctor instead. They took a sample of the stool and sent it to a laboratory. This was on Friday. By the end of the following week, I had not heard from the vet so I called. They had forgotten to send the sample they said.

Besides, the lab was closed for the weekend but no worry. William seemed fine now, didn't he? At that point he did. However, we had a trip to take. I had rented a U-Haul truck to deliver some furniture to my father's house in North Carolina. It was a long drive from Charlottesville, Virginia, to Spruce Pine, North Carolina. Of course, Sweet William was coming, but I also took along my daughter's Doberman. The whole drive down, William cuddled next to me on the seat. The Dobie stayed on the floor. We stopped twice at rest stops. Both times, William drank an entire bowl of water and seemed unwilling to saunter around the dog parks.

We arrived late, leaving the unloading until morning. William normally slept at the foot of my bed. That night, he chose not to and let the Dobie take his spot. In the morning, I woke up with a start. Something was wrong. I looked across the room and there was Sweet William leaning strangely against the wall. His eyes looked dazed so I approached him very quietly and slowly, afraid of frightening him. He was postured as if being tied against the wall, almost rigid. Not a comfortable position. When I reached out to pat his side, he cringed. Immediately I knew he was in pain. I called the vet and got his emergency number. He would meet us at the clinic.

The Doberman was left at the house while I ran across the street to borrow the neighbor's car to take William. Taking the U-Haul would have been impossible since it was still unpacked and the cab was far too high for a pup in pain. Coming down the neighbor's walkway, there was William walking very slowly up the hill just

to be with me. It was painful to watch. He would not
let me carry him. It was difficult getting him into the
car, but somehow I did as the tears welled up in my
eyes. Fortunately, the veterinary hospital was close. We
arrived in minutes. William was immediately placed on
the operating table and a tube was put in his side. He
was dehydrated and in severe pain. The doctor said he
could not determine the cause of his problem until the
pain was under control. He had more to say but I did
not hear him. I was focused on my brave little man lying
on the cold steel table. He asked that William be left
with him for the day and possibly the night so that he
could do some tests. I had no choice. I went home to the
Dobie and made myself busy unpacking the truck. In the
afternoon, I made a visit to the vet. William was in a cage
with an IV attached to his side. I spent about an hour on
my knees talking to him through the bars. His sweet
eyes focused on me and almost shifted back and forth
as if to say, "I'm all right. Please don't worry." The other
dogs in the clinic were respectfully silent. That evening,
my son and a friend came from college to help unload
the truck. We had no food in the house so we stopped to
have pizza and then went to the hospital. It was locked.
No visits possible with William until morning.

The boys chose sleeping bags to sleep by the fire
in the living room. I retired to the bedroom with Jessie,
the Dobie. The vet was supposed to call if there was any
change when he went that night to check the animals.
Nevertheless, even with Jessie at the foot of my bed, I
found it very hard to go to sleep. The lights were off
leaving only flickers from the fire reflecting on the walls

leading to the living room. Just as I was dozing off, Jessie leaped off the bed. She dashed into the living room and raced from one end to the other waking up the boys and terrifying me. Then, just as sudden, she came back to my room, jumped on the foot of the bed, curled up, and immediately fell fast asleep! Within seconds, the telephone rang. It was the veterinarian. William had just passed away.

When I told the doctor about Jesse's performance, he replied that he had heard of this kind of thing happening before. "You see," he said, "William just passed over to say goodbye."

The autopsy revealed that indeed the white stool had been a warning, though probably too late to do anything. The liver and kidney were practically non-existent. It was amazing he had lasted this long. We suspect he had raided a trash can in our Charlottesville neighborhood and a poison had been part of its contents. This poison had slowly eaten away his insides.

With the boys' help, we dug a grave on the hillside below the house. It was a lovely setting with overhanging trees and flowering bushes all around and a vista of the mountain peaks in the distance.

Although William's body is buried in North Carolina's Blue Ridge, we know his soul has moved on. Perhaps he'll come live with me again, but as another dog.

When my children were young, we inherited a little pup named Suzie-Q. Soon after coming into our family, she lost one leg in an automobile accident. We called her our three-legged wonder.

It all began when I was shopping near our home in Rolling Hills, California, on the Palos Verdes Peninsula just west and south of Los Angeles. It was summertime and the shopping area was packed with mothers and their children. With few parking spots near the grocery store, I chose to leave my car a block away in a shaded area. After making my purchases and loading them into the car, I saw a couple of kids walking a darling little puppy along the grassy area under the trees next to my car. Not able to resist a pat—after seeking permission of course—I asked the children to tell me about their dog. She was being sheltered at a veterinary hospital, they said. They had found the pup but because they lived in an apartment, they couldn't keep her. While they tried to locate a permanent home, the veterinary clinic agreed to board her for a minimal fee. We had two dogs at the time, but one look at this brave little face and I couldn't help but put her in the back seat of our car and take her home. Bigger and more robust, nevertheless, the other dogs immediately respected her; in fact, Suzie-Q became the leader of the pack. Then one day, she disappeared. Frantic, I ran down our driveway to the street fearing the worst. She was nowhere to be found. I knew she would not run away since she had become an integral part of our family. Once loyal, such a dog remains loyal. As for Suzy-Q, fidelity and devotion were her middle names. So I called my children and we organized a search all over the grounds which included a steep hillside sloping down to a canyon. Fortunately, she had not gone that far. My son found her hiding under some bushes close to the house. She was bleeding and upon closer examination, we found her right hind leg at an unnatural angle. Carefully, we placed her in the car and drove to the vet.

The leg had to be amputated. Apparently, Suzy-Q had been hit by a car, had made her way back up the steep driveway, was able to hobble to the garden behind the house and had curled up to die under the bush. I don't know why she didn't come to us for help, but we were all glad we found her in time. After surgery, she came home and spent a week living in the confined area of my bathroom before she was able to return to the pack.

For years she played with her canine companions and my children. She followed us when we rode the horses on the trails and was always included in any and all family functions. Her infirmity was never a hindrance. She learned to adjust her weight so the three legs could balance and kept up with her four legged and two legged pals. Our little wonder pup outlived both the other dogs. When it was her time to leave us, I was holding her in my arms.

It happened one late afternoon. I had come home close to dinner time after spending hours tending to one of our horses. At the foot of the stairs, I found our little miss lying on the floor. But she wasn't resting. Something was wrong. Her breathing was erratic as she struggled for each breath. When I called to her and she couldn't get up, I knew we had a problem. I had my daughter telephone the vet. We bundled Suzy-Q up and hurried to the hospital. Our doctor had agreed to meet us there since it was after hours and the hospital was closed. Suzie-Q was still gasping for breath but otherwise appeared peaceful as I embraced her on my lap and my daughter drove. After rushing us into the operating room and placing Suzy-Q on the operating table, the doctor left to get an oxygen tent. I held her little body pleading with her, "Don't leave us yet, sweet Suzie." The doctor had said Suzie-Q's lungs were filled with liquid.

Then something happened. It wasn't the movement. It wasn't her eyes that told me. Something ephemeral escaped, like a mist. It floated out of Suzy-Q and up to the right disappearing in the darkness of the ceiling. Though her limbs still moved, I knew. Suzy-Q had left us.

"Don't bother with the oxygen," I called out to the doctor, my voice cracking with grief. She came back into the room, examined my brave little lady and confirmed my diagnosis.

So, how do we measure intelligence? Empathy, compassion, endurance, and loyalty. With such standards, do you think people can measure up to dogs?

CHRISTIAN

The telephone rang in that seesaw aggravating and piercing way only French telephones can sound. It was five AM. I rolled over, picked up the receiver, mumbled "Oui," and a frantic male voice screamed at me. Come at once, he said. "Venez vite! Il n'y a pas une minute à perdre!" The "animal" was loose. Everyone was "terrorized" (he did not mince his words even if this is a translation). "Il s'est enfui de la cage. C'est pas possible ça! On a d'autre chose à faire!" he yelled through the speaker. And with a sigh, "Ah! ces Americains!" he hung up.

When I left Washington, it was ostensibly to have a little vacation in Europe. Christian was placed in a kennel. But after several weeks in Paris, I decided to totally immerse myself in the French lifestyle for a year. I rented an apartment in Sèvre and sent for my companion, Christian.

There was a large screened-in area, like a huge cage, at Orly airport containing unclaimed boxes and baggage and today, one frightened young German Shepherd. When I called him, Christian ran up to me, tail wagging and tongue licking and so loving and grateful for my presence that it really made the airport stewards look foolish. These big Frenchmen had not dared to enter the 'cage' and many irate passengers were impatiently waiting for their bags.

I did not realize it then, but my entire stay in Europe would revolve around this young pup. It was the beginning of a series of adventures I have had throughout the years, always involving a pet.

Christian came home to my apartment outside Paris. He was one worn out dog suffering from a major bout of jet lag. As the days passed, I took him everywhere and the French people were wonderful with him. He was allowed in cafés, in taxis, almost everywhere except museums.

Then one day he began to throw up. I took him to the vet. Some pills were prescribed. I also realized he never recouped the energy he had before his flight across the ocean.

The medicine did not seem to alleviate Christian's lethargy. In France, at least in those days, nature was prescribed as often as pills. Whole stores were devoted to the sale of bottled waters. The bottles were assembled according to their curative characteristics. To the uninformed, such a store looked like a wine shop. Christian had his special waters but still no change. Next on the list of natural cures was a change of environment. If the patient had been human, a spa would have been recommended. In our case, the two options were either the sea or the South.

I had a great Uncle living in Rome. The only American Canon of St. Peter's, Great-Uncle William refused to live behind the walls of the Vatican. Instead he had an apartment (replete with chapel) in the Palazzo Doria. Needless to say, Christian and I could not stay with my uncle, but arrangements were made for us to sublet an apartment nearby.

I still have Christian's train ticket. It was a long ride from Paris to Rome made longer by the fact that I had to quickly exit the train with my friend every time it came to a stop worried lest he make a mess in our cabin.

After getting settled in Rome, my first priority was to take Christian to a vet. The outcome of this visit was the diagnosis of both heart worms and tuberculosis. The doctor said we must first kill the heart worms and then, if he survived, deal with the TB. His diet for the former was pasta. This would be the worst diet for the TB but absolutely necessary for getting rid of the worms.

During this regime, we walked twice daily in a fresh unpolluted area. Thanks to my great-uncle's landlords, the Principessa and Dom Doria, we had access to one of the Seven Hills of Rome. The Doria family owned one of the most beautiful villas and gardens that I have ever seen. Presenting my pass at the gate, I and my "persona d'accompagno" had free access to miles of the Doria Pamphini gardens and fields. Reflection ponds, fountains, tall Italian Cypress trees, and fields of manicured grass were all ours alone for the afternoon. Alone, that is, until one day Christian ran off, barking wildly. Behind the trees, down the hill, was a herd of sheep. Before I could catch up with him, Christian had separated one unsuspecting sheep from the herd. Thinking he had seen a wolf, the sheep panicked. Running up the hill, he must have had a heart attack. I found him upside down, legs straight up and very dead. All of a sudden, from down below, came a voice yelling I hated to think what. It was the shepherd who tended the herd. Now we were in real trouble! I grabbed Christian and fearfully awaited the man. Breathlessly, he came up the hill, surveyed his sheep, and then, to my astonishment, shrugged his shoulders. "Una sigaretta americana?" he asked. Boy was I glad to comply!

Of course, Christian could never shed his "disguise." The Romans knew a wolf when they saw one. "Cane loupo, cane loupo" someone would yell and a whole block of people would run across the street leaving my shepherd and me with an empty sidewalk. If you are in a hurry in Rome, this certainly has its advantages.

Christian improved, regaining some of the spark and stamina of old. We had passed the worm test. Now the diet was changed to beat the TB. Meat replaced the pasta. But the battle was far from won. To help our side, I planned a little trip.

We drove to Assisi; to the Basilica di S. Francesco; or to be precise, to the front pew in front of the altar in the church of the patron saint of animals. The basilica was dark. Candls flickered near the entrance and a pale light shone over the cross above the altar. But to the tourists who came in the narthex or posterior of the church, the two little ears sticking up from the front pew were visible enough to recognize and clearly not human. The guide told me later that he was sure St. Francis was pleased to have Christian in his church, especially a dog so aptly named.

Several months later, we boarded a ship in Naples, once again to cross the Atlantic, but this time in a more leisurely fashion. No more frantic episodes in airports for either of us! Besides, the trip home was strictly first class; at least, it was first class plus for Christian. The kennels were on the top deck while my cabin was several levels below in economy class.

Going through customs in New York, I smiled sweetly, handed my credentials to the officer and then, feigning an embarrassing moment if Christian didn't get to some grass soon, was able to practically run through the process. Should they find out about Christian's illnesses, I thought, he might not be allowed back in the U.S. When we finally returned to Washington, I called the vet and made an appointment. X-rays were taken. It appeared that every internal organ was scared or deformed in some way. The doctor said this indicated some serious illnesses. He was amazed that the dog had survived. "Today," he said, "despite all that has gone before, I give Christian a clean bill of health." Thank you, St. Francis.

IN HONOR OF
JOHN CROSBY

The cup was delicate, almost transparent, very old,
and probably quite valuable. I raised it carefully, the
steam rising, the aroma as mild as the cup was fragile.
Slowly I brought the cup to my lips. Having come this
far, holding the cup so far from its saucer and so close
to my mouth, I would have to take a sip careful not to
slurp but also careful not to burn my mouth. Between
the fragile cup and the hot tea, I was glad my hand was
steady. In the background behind and beyond this still-
life of a cup and a hand was the blurred face of my host.
It was like a photograph taken at the wrong setting for
distance. My eyes were focused on my hand, the cup,
and the tea not daring to look at John.

Then my hand began to shake. I must take that sip and somehow gracefully put the cup back down in its saucer without spilling. As the sweat accumulated under my armpits and my stomach did a flip flop, I successfully deposited the tea cup.

This whole episode lasted only a few seconds; but for me, those few seconds represented a long lasting moment, a memorable moment when my decision became clear. It was the focal point of my first encounter with John Crosby. Despite my timidity and the episode with the tea, I had survived meeting a man who was the first television critic to achieve fame. Before television, John had been a popular radio critic. He had written for *The New York Herald Tribune* on both sides of the Atlantic plus he had authored over fifteen books. As a result of becoming personally acquainted with this living legend, I made an important decision. Choosing the 'path less traveled,' I decided to become a writer.

It was only a couple of months ago (this was written in 1991-ed) that I learned about John's condition. I remember the day he came to the shop where his wife, Kate, manufactured Dionis Goat's Milk soap products in Charlottesville, Virginia. He drove up in his old beat-up Datsun. After a brief chat and look about, he had to sit and rest before he could get back into the car and drive home to their little farm in the country. That was to be the last time he would be allowed to drive himself.

Two weeks ago, I was asked to come to the farm to bed sit. The hospice care people came earlier in the afternoon. They assisted John from his bed to the bath, remade his bed and then tucked him in securely. On the table next to the headboard was a glass of water and a straw. John was in a rented hospital bed placed in what used to be the downstairs dining room. When I arrived, the hospice people were leaving and said John was sleeping. From the corridor, I could hear his respiration; it was raspy. Peeking through the door, I could see his whole body rising and falling with each breath. With a deep sigh, I grit my teeth and entered the room on tiptoe. John's eyes opened a slit and, in a hoarse whisper, he asked for some tea. I hoped that my smile belied my shock seeing his distinguished form reduced to loose flesh and bone. He could not get up. I went to the kitchen and heated the pot, poured hot water over the tea bag, added some goat's milk and honey, found a straw, and brought the cup back into the dining room. It was an effort just to raise him up on the pillows so he could take his tea through the straw. I didn't know what to say. It was hard to tell how much he understood. I also didn't know whether he was too tired just trying to live a little longer to even care about what I said, so we both remained silent except for the slow sipping through the straw. When he closed his eyes, I let him fall gently back onto the pillow and then tiptoed out.

The library was just across the hall, well within hearing distance. On the tables were photographs of John and his family. Paintings they had collected from different parts of the world hung on the walls. On the shelves were row upon row of John's own books along with many of his and Kate's old favorites. I chose one of John's I hadn't heard about before. It had been published in London early in his career. Book in hand, I checked the dining room. John appeared to be sleeping so I sat down and began to read. John's breathing was labored but there was nothing I could do. Reading his own written words was the only dialogue I would have with John.

The phone rang. It was Kate. She would be late but, she advised, go ahead and leave. "John will be fine alone," she said. I hung up the phone and came back into the room. John's eyes were open.

"That was Kate. She said she would be a bit late."

"Don't leave. Please don't leave me," he whispered.

I had no intention of leaving. Clearly John was going to die. Maybe not tonight, but soon. He was terrified of dying alone. I would stay.

There was much concern about where to place the flower arrangement. If it was put in front of the podium, it would block out the minister's face. If it was placed behind the podium, it would be blocked by the minister. Nevertheless, the consensus was that it should be there in front of the gathering. Finally, it was placed on the left which was amusing considering John's politics. However, it was on the minister's right which was most appropriate for him. John would think so; of that I was sure.

The guests continued to arrive bringing food and grief or, at the very least, compassion. I was in charge of the food table which was rearranged almost every time a guest arrived. Three times it had to be moved to avoid the bright rays of the descending sun. It was a beautiful, bright, warm early fall afternoon in the central Virginia countryside. The tent had been placed near John's swimming pool (paid for, he had once confided, by the republishing of *Contract on the President*). The house was to the south of the tent. The pastures for their three horses paralleled both sides of the entrance drive which was full of potholes from several rough winters and no repair. The goats lived in their own quarters beyond and behind the farmhouse.

I glanced over at the podium wondering when the minister was going to begin. He was still pacing back and forth. Probably collecting his thoughts. Then I noticed the flower arrangement. It had acquired a resident. On a leaf in the back, sat, unperturbed and arrogant as you please, a butterfly. How nice, I thought more intent upon looking for Kate. She and the family had taken the chairs in the front row. Her son's fiancé was asked to sit with them but declined gracefully and sat behind. Kate sat in the middle, a little to the right of the podium. Her posture was so erect, so still, so, as John liked to point out, British. John had said that he used to watch Kate from the upstairs bedroom window as she went about her chores. He loved watching the way she walked, "like a woman going somewhere, full of purpose, erect, determined, not only to get (where she was going) but to accomplish whatever she has in mind…. It's all there in that fearfully British stride," he wrote in his memoirs.

Waking from my reverie, I glanced at the flower arrangement. The butterfly had moved. He was on the front leaf now. He wasn't eating, sniffing, or whatever butterflies do. He was just perched, proud and somewhat

defiant. Other people were beginning to notice him. I
overheard some muffled phrases here and there and
wondered if Kate noticed. The minister cleared his
throat. The service was about to begin. The butterfly
clearly intended to stay.

The minister, also a neighbor of Kate and John's,
was an Episcopalian. He was also of the Buddhist
philosophical persuasion. It was his philosophy not his
faith that would dictate the service. John was an atheist.
Kate had instructed the minister not to mention God.

The minister/philosopher was quite candid
when he spoke about the deceased. "He was a man
of extremes," he began. He talked about John's quick
temper followed by his just as quick gentleness. I had
to admit feeling a bit ill at ease with all this candidness.
I looked over at Kate but she seemed unmoved, sitting
erect and still. Kate had said she wanted a service John
would have enjoyed. So all this honesty was part of the
program. I looked at the butterfly as if to confirm my
opinion.

Then it came to me. In a flash of understanding, I
knew: The butterfly was John! He simply could not miss
his last party. How else could the creature's behavior be
explained? The butterfly seemed to be staring at the
gathering, checking out their reactions, one face at a
time. That was John, always observing.

The minister talked on and on. Not that he was
boring, certainly not, but he did seem to ramble. This
was John's memorial service. The minister seemed
to forget his objective, I thought, reflecting about the
man I so admired. An atheist, John had lived hard. A

journalist, John had observed and recorded, missing little. A novelist, John had spun tales of adventure and intrigue. Very masculine. Born in 1912, John had lived through and participated in a unique era, an era of extremes. Two World Wars on either side of the extremes of the twenties and thirties. An era of excess wealth displayed lavishly (with no income tax) followed by the Depression. John was there; he had experienced it all. He had been to Pamplona with Hemingway. He had been treated like royalty in the capitals of Europe. As a reporter, he had initiated the radio reviews and later the television reviews in the *Herald*. And through it all, John Crosby observed and wrote. Instinctively, I looked at the butterfly. "Isn't that right, John?"

I wasn't sure when he left, the butterfly that is. People were starting to get up. I had to reset the table one more time for the buffet. When I finally had a chance to look at the flower arrangement, the butterfly was gone. "Did you enjoy the party, John?" I asked knowing full well what the answer would be.

SHAWNARA

*Love will find the solution within itself to every problem,
will answer every question. It is the lodestone of Life, the
center of Reality, the heart of the Universe, and it will
ultimately win and vanquish every foe.*

ERNEST HOLMES

In some special way, I know people and animals
communicate. Not all people and not all animals. But
when it happens, it is very real and very intense. I have
had this experience with many of my dogs, horses, a goat,
and even, when they permit, my cats. One incidence,
though painfully poignant, stands out.

Shawnara was a half quarter horse, half Arab
mare. She taught all my children to ride but for me,
she was therapy. When I needed to get away from the
house and three small children, I would hop on her
bareback and ride the trails. Sometimes we would go
out for two or three hours at a time. The dogs would
follow along but it was really just the two of us enjoying
each other's company and the land we were riding
through. We would mutually agree when to canter or
trot or just amble along. When the children rode her,
she would be mindful of the small body on her back and

walk slowly, stopping if they were off-balance. She was
the kind of horse you felt you could bring into the house
and she would behave as one of the family. And truly
she was. This went on for years until one day, we had
to move. The preceding year, for no apparent reason,
Shawnara had become anxious about traveling in the
trailer. She would kick and rear up when we tried to
load her. If we got her in, she would lean against the
side. This is terrifying for the driver (myself) and just
plain dangerous. We were moving from California to
Connecticut. Beside the discomfort the trip would
cause, I was afraid since she was advanced in years, the
never before experienced cold winters would be bad for
her. So I gave Shawnara to a friend who had a nice stable
and a riding ring. Turnout paddocks of any size are rare
in Southern California, but I was assured she would be
turned out in the ring and trail ridden regularly. I will
never forget the look she gave me when I left her in the
friend's ring that day.

Every year, I would fly back to California to visit and ride my old friend. Then one day I received a call. My former neighbor, Pam, who raised Saddle bred0 horses, said she wanted to bring Shawnara to her farm.

She was not being properly cared for, Pam said. The people were not riding her and she was not being kept in a stall but instead in a tiny outdoor port-a-fence paddock without protection. Her hay was being thrown on the ground which was sand and she was getting stiff from being in such cramped quarters. I was grateful for my neighbor's concern and was only too happy to give her permission to bring Shawnara to her farm.

Several months later, I decided to fly out to California. It was a spur of the moment decision. When I arrived at the airport, I was met by a very grim-faced Pam. My worst fears were realized. While I was on the plane crossing the continent, Shawnara had gone down in her stall. The vet had come and given her an injection to relieve the pain. He was returning the next day to do exploratory surgery. A blocked intestine was suspected. The sand!

That evening and the next morning I spent soothing my old friend. Pam was instructed to shave her side for surgery. It was a hideous sight, more because of what it stood for than the way it looked. I hugged Shawnara and she gave me one of those looks.

The vet arrived. Pam held Shawnara who was heavily sedated. I could not watch. I kissed my old mare on the nose knowing that it was goodbye and went inside the house to wait for the results. An hour went by. I prayed that my instincts were wrong, that she could be saved. But then Pam came in to the living room and said there was nothing that Dr. Kelly could do. Although I had no choice, it was my responsibility to give permission and allow Shawnara to die.

She had waited for me to come home to say goodbye.

There is no logical explanation for her knowing I was flying back to California. I had not even planned that trip. But Shawnara knew I was coming. I loved that mare and I pray that she will forgive me for leaving her behind.

If we listen, our animals will teach us more about love than most of our fellow human friends can or will.

HUGS AND KISSES

Whenever an animal is somehow forced into the service of men, every one of us must be concerned for any suffering it bears on that account. No one of us may permit any preventable pain to be inflicted, even though the responsibility is not ours. No one may appease his conscience by thinking he would be interfering in something that does not concern him. No one may shut his eyes and think the pain, which is therefore not visible to him, is non-existent.

ALBERT SCHWEITZER

He was big from what I could tell looking into his small, dark, untidy stall. Going around and around in circles within his confined area, the horse was clearly needing attention. I asked to have him brought outside so I could look at him more carefully and possibly get on him to ride about the place.

Once outside, I could see Hughey was beautiful. A 16.3 hand gelding, his chestnut hair and his flaxen mane and tail reflected his Belgian heritage and his tall, thin legs and small feet reflected the thoroughbred side. He was happy to be out in the sun and particularly pleased to be allowed to nibble the grass while my husband held him loosely by a lead rope. I went to the car to fetch my saddle and bridle, came back, saddled him up and took him or allowed him to take me on a tour of the property. At a trot, his gait was comfortable, nice long strides, smooth and graceful. His canter was a charm, floating over the ground, head down, relaxed, no tension and loose reins.

So Hughey came home with us. The family who owned him had no idea of his age. We had our vet come check him and she guessed he was about 18 years old. The horse had been purchased for a preteen-aged girl to show in Children's and Junior Hunter Divisions. In the beginning, she won many ribbons on Hughey whose show name was Hugs and Kisses. But as she entered her teen years, riding took less of a precedent. Hughey's happiness was no longer her top priority. At the end, he was totally ignored. Although the family was paying what I consider a fortune to board this kind horse, he was only being turned out for three hours a day and rarely ridden. His feet were overdue for being shod and his stall was only cleaned once a day. A miserable life.

Hughey adjusted easily to our small farm life. Mr. Luke, my husband's quarter horse, and he became great pals, grazing together, nickering at each other when in their stalls, splashing water about in the trough and playing follow-the-other's-tail in circles on the grass. Two or three times a week, my husband and I took the horses out on trail rides near our farm as well as several rides through the Manassas Battlefields. Once we participated in a rated trail ride up a mountain and down with judged obstacles along the way. Hughey was almost perfect on the obstacles but the trail up and down was far more than we had anticipated, so we slowed down to allow our elderly horses to catch their breath and relax. We won no ribbons but had an enjoyable day nevertheless. Once I took Hughey to a small, local horse show. He was excited. But it was a nervous excitement, a bit out-of-control, and although we placed, we were far down the line from the blue ribbons.

Hughey had a wonderful smile. He would put his head on my shoulder, nuzzle me and then give me one of those happy, contented looks, a smile with teeth showing and eyes twinkling. When he finished his meals, he would stick out his tongue between his teeth as if cleaning any leftover grains that might be caught in his gum. That was a sight I wish I had caught on camera.

Whenever we had guests, it was Hughey who stuck his head out of his stall to say hi. He loved attention and he was an expert at giving back love.

Wednesday, Mr. Hughey gave up his life. Horses are tough. In the wild, they can't show any pain or they will be attacked. Domesticated, they still retain the solid demeanor even when they are dying. The prior Sunday, we had called the vet in when he showed signs of bowel upset. He also had a fever of 104. She suspected severe gas, cleaned his intestines out, gave him an injection, waited for his fever to subside and took a blood sample. The initial results showed that he was anemic but any further analysis would take time. Twice a day for three days, Dr. French and her assistant came to check on Hughey, to reach up for bowel movement under his tail, to insert a tube in his nostril that descended to his stomach and to take his pulse. My husband and I were told to take his temperature every few hours and to only feed him a handful of hay if we found a stool. Since he couldn't graze, the pasture was closed to him. So Tuesday evening, in addition to his stall and runway, we gave him the sacrifice area around the barn. This would allow him room to roam a bit. Walking about would hopefully help his digestive system. The other horses were turned out in their pastures but within sight of Hughey. Sadly, in the morning, there was no sign of a bowel movement. Hughey was playing with the water, but not drinking much. I offered him some pellets but he showed no interest. The vet came, checked him again and decided he should continue being observed but that there was little concern since he seemed otherwise in pretty good shape. I wasn't there but this is what my husband reported. When I came home, I changed into jeans and went down to the barn. He was throwing himself down on the stall floor. Then up for a moment and down again. No whining or whinnying. But obvious pain. The vet was called. We were able to get Hughey outside, but once in the pasture, he threw himself down again and we couldn't get him up. I checked his mouth. His gums were dry. We took his temperature. 103.7 and rising. He was in severe pain. When the vet arrived, we had a decision to make. No, that isn't true. Hughey had made his decision; we simply needed to help him make his transition less painful. I held his head, told him I loved him as he peacefully left us. It took awhile for his body to loose its energy but Hughey was gone. Hugs and Kisses, goodbye. We will always love you.

Mr. Hughey is buried behind Mr. Woodstock who you will meet in another chapter. Two special souls, now free, without bondage.

(See my Biography page for a photo of Hughey.)

Hoof Tails

Imagine being born in one of the most prestigious farms in Kentucky with a famous dam and sire, bred to race. Imagine being double crossed (inbred) with Nashua in your pedigree. Of course, you win a sizable amount of money for your owners at places like Hollywood Park and Santa Anita in the west, and then come east to race at Pimlico, and finally, age six, to Virginia and race at Colonial Downs. You fall and are injured. You should be given proper medical care. Instead, your owners stick you in an auction.

This is Just'n's story. He is not unique. Although I grew up in Washington, DC and La Jolla, California,, my love of horses has taken me and my family into the country where we could have horses on our property. In 1972, then a single parent of three small children, I inherited a thoroughbred mare. After interviewing trainers and barn managers, I decided to breed my mare to a famous stallion. I chose Petrone. Although the odds were practically 100% against me since there was nothing notable about my mare, neither her lineage nor her own racing career, I was blessed. In 1976, the foal, a filly whom I name Patty Petrone, was second in her first race at Santa Anita and proceeded to win her second race. These wins were followed by more at Hollywood Park and Del Mar where she bowed a tendon. After this final valiant effort, coming in a photo finish on the turf for third place, she was retired. Later I bred her resulting in another winner named Risky Ronnie. However, a few years later, when my trainer, the late Eddie Gregson, told me not to come to the back stretch because, he said, I would not want to know what some owners were doing to their horses, I quit. It was not until 2009 that thoroughbred horses were forbidden to race "under the influence": steroids. Shocking that it took so long. No longer racing or showing thoroughbreds, instead I am rescuing these dear souls.

Back to Just'n, a name we gave the Kentucky born race horse, as in an old song's lyrics: "Just in time; we found you just in time..." A lovely 16.3 hand thoroughbred, he was purchased for only $100.00. Here is his story.

A neighbor had heard about an eight year old, registered thoroughbred gelding being sold for a ridiculously small sum of money. He simply had to go see for himself why. He drove over the Blue Ridge from Virginia to West Virginia. When he arrived at a remote homestead in the hills, he could not believe his eyes. There in a round pen with a hay bale in the middle was a skinny dark brown horse and two cows. The owners explained that they had tried to make this thoroughbred race horse into a barrel racer. Of course it didn't work. This pathetic animal was not only emaciated, his hooves were pointed upward from no farrier work. You could only guess what his teeth looked like. Clearly, they had no idea how to care for a thoroughbred horse. Without hesitation, the neighbor decided to bring him home. His wife said when the horse exited the trailer she could not believe what she saw. Even his glassy eyes told her this was a horse ready to accept an early demise. Every bone in his body showed through the taut skin. He was a walking skeleton, she said.

After a few months of proper care, he called and offered this horse to me because, he said, he knew I would give him the good home he deserved. When he arrived, we lifted his lip, read his tattoo, and did the research. This I how we discovered his racing history. He had won a sizable amount of money in the beginning racing at the same tracks as my late Patty Petrone but then slowed down. My initial guess was that he was simply given away when he no longer performed. That is, until we found a real reason. When I observed him limping after galloping around the pasture with the other horses, I asked for X-rays to be taken. A bone chip was located in his right front leg. Had he undergone surgery when this injury occurred, he would be sound now. However, the owners must have decided he was not worth the expense. They simply threw him into the sale. After all, he is a gelding so there was, in their selfish opinion, no future earning potential. No thought of the time and effort this dedicated, well-bred horse had undergone racing for over four years. All for the owners' pocketbook. I wish he could share his stories with me. No, maybe I don't. Happily, for him at least, his fate is positive unlike so many hard working, big hearted horses who are literally disposed of (many sold as meat to Europe) following an unsuccessful career.

Postscript

We acquired another rescue soon after bringing Just'n home. Prince, also a registered thoroughbred, had been left in a field with two other horses for over a year. His owner had died and her husband knew nothing about horses. Leaving them in a field, he thought, was perfectly alright. But one look at the three horses and anyone could see this was not the solution. By the time winter arrived, there was no grass left in the field. All three horses became emaciated. When they were finally rescued by my vet, two were at death's door, one was skinny but still in fairly good shape. My vet called and said that the one horse named Prince was meant to be with me. "I don't know why, but I think he should be yours." When we went to her barn to pick him up, she warned us not to look in the first stall. Prince came onto our trailer willingly, but I did take a peek in that stall as we walked out of the barn. I have never seen such a skeletal specimen. I had to look away quickly but my tears gave me away. How anyone could allow such a travesty? This poor fellow died two days later.

Meanwhile, Prince became part of our equine family. He gained weight and began to show us what he could do. He loves to jump and will jump anything and probably any height. Just'n tends to be a bit bossy, but Prince tolerates Just'n's behavior and is happy to graze next to him and follow him around the pasture.

Now both horses not only have security; they have a job. On a nice day, we take them trail riding. My son prefers riding Just'n bareback. Prince also does additional ring work while Just'n watches. As he trots or canters around the ring, every now and then Prince will glance over to see if his buddy approves. For us, watching their enjoyment and their renewed energy is one of the great rewards. Truly, to give is to receive, but what we receive from these fellows is far more than what we have to give.

> *Whenever an animal is somehow forced into the service of men, every one of us must be concerned for any suffering it bears on that account. No one of us may permit any preventable pain to be inflicted, even though the responsibility is not ours. No one may appease his conscience by thinking he would be interfering in something that does not concern him. No one may shut his eyes and think the pain, which is therefore not visible to him, is non-existent.*

ALBERT SCHWEITZER

MASTER WOODSTOCK

I'm a lean dog, a keen dog, a wild dog and lone.
IRENE RUTHERFORD MCLEOD
Songs to Save a Soul, 1919

We will never know where he was born or how he came to Woodstock Farm in Albemarle County, Virginia. A little ball of fur, a mere handful of starving pup, he was following the heels of grazing cows, no doubt hoping for a drink. The cows kicked him away; he persisted. That pup was a survivor. We brought him home, fed him, took him to the vet, and a few months later, he became a yacht pup. He was one loving, loyal, and smart sailor.

Becoming a yacht pup did not happen overnight but it did not take long. As soon as he was on board the boat, he acknowledged it as home. Sure-footed as he was, there was no question of his falling overboard nor did he make any attempt to jump. The first day, he learned how to swim with a life vest made from placing a child's vest upside down across his back and under his belly. We dropped anchor out at sea and had to literally release him into the water. Of course he was frightened

but I was swimming alongside to grab or coax him along.
He was not pleased but he did swim. We hauled him up
the swimming steps onto the ramp protruding behind
the boat, disrobed him, and both he and the vest were
hosed off before he could climb up the next level to the
main deck. This routine became a daily ritual, but not
that first night since we returned to the dock. The next
day was for real.

It was late afternoon before the breeze became
enough of a wind to give us momentum. Our sailboat,

42 foot Jeanneau, has an engine but it has not worked since we left the Dominican Republic. We rely entirely on the whim of the wind. This has been an amazingly windless summer so our progress has been slow. Captain Sandy and I had sailed seventeen hundred miles without the engine. We were glad to finally reach the mainland of Florida. It was much longer than we anticipated and we needed to be in U.S. waters before we could retrieve Woodstock.

As we left the channel of Cape Canaveral, the so-called 'wind' diminished. What had taken a half hour the day before took three and a half hours today and this just to get out of the channel to the ocean! It was already dark. As we sailed through the night, I worried about Woodstock. He must need to go to the bathroom. He treated the boat like his home and would not allow himself to make a mess. In vain, we tried to encourage him. I won't even discuss some of the ways we tried. I'm sure he was not oblivious of our intentions, just stubborn in his opposition.

By morning, it was clear: he would have to be taken ashore. Thus began the pattern which would cause us to take weeks instead of days to travel up the East coast. We could not get on the 'Atlantic Express' (the Gulf Stream) and ride it north because we needed to hug the coast to accommodate Master Woodstock.

Our sailboat has a draft of six and a half feet. This limits just how close we can sail to the shore before dropping anchor. The first morning, the distance to shore was quite far. We learned a lot that first day.

We put Woodstock's vest on. Not pleased, he was none the less tolerant. Sandy pulled in the dingy, which had been bobbing along behind the boat. We threw in the oars and then I got in. Sandy handed over the bewildered pup. With Woodstock in the middle, I sat at the bow with an oar and Sandy took to the rear with the other oar. We untied the line and started rowing. Now keep in mind that we are rowing *to* the shore; therefore, we could almost ride the tide and surf onto the beach.

And surf we did. The little white foam we had seen from the boat became very large, serious waves as we approached our destination.

"Keep rowing," yelled Sandy over the roar of the surf. I looked back over my shoulder. There was a huge wave descending upon us. "Row!" he yelled again.

"But look…," I attempted. The wave crashed down and we went under. The dingy, now sideways because of my not rowing, flipped over.

"Where's Woodstock?" I sputtered after coming up for air.

"Under the dingy!"

We lifted the dingy even as the waves pounded down on us, the surf pushing us ashore. Poor little Woodstock. In the dark, under the shell of the dingy, he was paddling frantically. He looked miserable, but he was alive and afloat with the help of the vest. Neither a whimper nor a yelp, no complaint came from our little man as we pushed him along through the water to the shore. Off came the vest and off went the pup. Relief at last!

That was one happy dog. Instantly forgetting his ordeal with the dingy, he scampered off, relieved himself and then allowed his natural instincts to revive. There were birds to flush so with his tail extended, he ran up and down the beach in hot pursuit.

Eventually it was time to return to the boat. How to do this? We tried pushing the dingy with Woodstock inside through the waves. But, one look at the white frothy mountains descending on him and he leaped out of the dingy into the water front feet paddling like a windmill at full speed and headed for shore.

Next, Sandy took the dingy out beyond the waves leaving me to swim out and through the waves with Woodstock. My little man was petrified and I was not strong enough to hold him up as the waves crashed down on the two of us. We retreated to the beach. Poor Sandy had to come back with the dingy. Exhausted, the three of us sat on the sand, staring at the waves, the sea, and the boat anchored beyond and tried to devise a plan.

Finally Capt. Sandy came up with an idea. He would take the dingy back to the sailboat; get a small anchor, another vest, and a long line. It was a tough trip negotiating the waves again and rowing alone against the tide out to the boat.

However, this plan worked. We attached Woodstock to the second vest at the end of the long line. The dingy was anchored behind the waves. It was arduous but successful. Woodstock was literally dragged through the surf, under the wave and up to the far side. We raised him out of the water and with no reluctance he flopped over the side and into the dingy. Then we faced the long row, the Captain's third, back to the boat. This day's expedition lasted over four hours. Obviously we had to modify the next outing or we would never get anywhere, wind or no wind.

Our trip from Cape Canaveral, Florida, to Wrightsville Beach, North Carolina, lasted almost four weeks instead of a few days. That portion of our voyage ended in the wake of Hurricane Emily. The return to Annapolis was postponed.

We have many tales to tell, but our star, our protagonist, our main joy is this young pup from Albemarle County, Virginia. He has changed our lives and we have changed his. Just don't let anyone tell you that a country pup can't become a great sailor!

DEDICATED TO MR. WOODSTOCK

There is a land of the living and
A land of the dead
And the bridge is love
The only survival, the only meaning.
THORNTON WILDER

He was Master Woodstock until he turned nine, then he became Mister Woodstock. He also became so immersed in my life that being called my shadow was only part of the story. From a lost and starving pup found in the woods south of Charlottesville, Virginia, to a master sailor, to my "assistant" when I was teaching, Woodstock was always there. And he wasn't there as a bother. He was a support. But he was also next to me for protection. If there was a loud noise, like thunder, he would shake uncontrollably and seek my arms. If he was in an unfamiliar place, he would trail my feet, inches away from every step. So it was a mutual attachment. I needed him and he needed me.

Our relationship began when I was single. My children were pretty much on their own. My dog, Sweet William, had been poisoned and died. I had my children's cat, Butch, but as much as I loved the big guy, I missed having a dog. Then this pup was presented to me. When I went to meet the little fellow, I wasn't sure at first so I sank down on my knees to have an eye to eye look and chat. But he was quick. Before both my knees were on the ground, he put his little paws around my neck. That sealed the deal. He was only six weeks old.

As soon as he came home with me, Butch took an immediate liking to the new baby and became Mr. Mom. Woodstock learned to purr and lick himself as any feline would do. It was a few years before he was sure about his identity as a pup not a cat. It was also awhile before we could identify his breed. Not knowing who his parents were and why he was found in a cow pasture following the big beasts around and being kicked at, we could only guess. His coloring and the contour of his face and his actions, sniffing and pointing, were pointer. His rear and body size, however, were hound. So, when asked, I would reply, he is a pure bred Pointer-hound, a true Virginia gentleman.

Together he and I hiked the battlefields of Virginia, the Blue Ridge Mountains, and when I was with a friend on a sailing trip, he became a first mate. He also became my grand daughter's guardian, never leaving her side when we went out for walks.

When I moved to California, he copiloted the big Penske truck I drove across country. Well, that's not true. Mr. Mom, had to be caged for the trip. Because the cab of the truck only had one seat and because of the size of the cage, there really was no room for Woodstock except on the floor. When we ran out of gas in the middle of the desert, Woodstock was standing beside me as I tried to wave down some help from the passing cars. We waited for hours until a police car spotted us. It was a frightening experience but Woodstock had confidence in a proper outcome.

In California, we joined a dog group and helped establish a dog park. Again, we hiked everywhere but his favorite spot was dog beach in Del Mar. He was a veritable flirt with the lady pups and loved romping through the surf.

When I was reunited with my first beau, my very first love senior year of high school, Woodstock was there. He was a real gentleman about this new person coming into my life. Not jealous, he just waited patiently for Steele to give him some attention too. And he did. Steele understood dogs. He and his daughters had raised CCI (Canine Companions for Independence) pups and he was anxious that Woodstock get together with his current companion, a yellow lab named Shadelin. It was quickly organized that the two boys meet. We planned a trip up the California coast, the four of us. Shadelin and Woodstock enjoyed each other's company but their personalities and interests were so different there was never competition between them. Shadelin likes to play ball. Woodstock could care less. Woodstock loved to hike and sniff, Shadelin had no idea what sniffing was all about.

Steele and I were married and bought a house in La Jolla, CA, the town where we both had grown up. My Virginia gentleman adjusted to being a California lad and both dogs were included in the many vacations taken in Steele's camper. Up and down the west coast including lovely long walks on the broad, empty beaches of Oregon, into the heart of the desert (this time with enough fuel because Steele was in charge!), walks down the streets of old deserted mining towns, through the Redwood Forest, under the Golden Gate Bridge, into the Muir Woods. Later, we explored the rest of the United States and parts of Canada. Woodstock loved the adventure. In Washington, DC, he and Shadelin posed with Franklin Delano Roosevelt and his Scottie, Fala, at the newly opened FDR Memorial, the only memorial in the nation's capital where dogs are allowed. So many places, so many experiences, I wonder how many tales he is telling his new friends now?

Yes, Mr. Woodstock has gone on. We returned to Virginia a little over two years ago. And these past two years were exciting for Woodstock since the smells were familiar and may have brought back memories of his youth. At the same time, we became aware that our little man was beginning to fail. His back legs weren't obeying his commands and often he needed assistance going over logs since he couldn't leap over anymore. He still jumped up on the side of our bed for a goodnight pat or a good morning lick, but even this was getting difficult and hard to sustain. We tried hydrotherapy, acupuncture, and several vets, but the problem was neurological and progressive and there was no cure. Slowly but increasingly, he was loosing the feel of his hind quarters. He had trouble with stairs. Then he began to loose control of his bowel movements. He was forced to wear a diaper, an embarrassment I am sure, but he resigned himself to the routine. Little by little, the distance he could walk was diminished. His eyes were glazy, his hearing diminished. He was fourteen.

My son said if we want to avoid death, we need to have turtles as pets. *The Washington Post* had an article recently about a turtle who died. Why would this be an event for newspaper publication? Because the turtle was at least 250 years old.

This was not a decision I wanted to make, but Mr. Woodstock was probably in pain and surely didn't want to revert to medications. He also missed being able to keep up with Shadelin and the two year old pup my husband had adopted from the Humane Society. To take walks with us became more and more of an effort until finally he said no, I can't go that far and we turned back. In the morning, he still accompanied the other two dogs to fetch the newspaper, supervised the procedure and returned to receive a treat. He also continued to come down to the barn and supervise the feeding and grooming of the horses. And he still to the last day came along side the tractor as I scooped up the manure from the field. But back in the house, he would slide on the floor, his hind legs sprawled out behind him, and cry for help. He would also slide down the stairs so I had to assist and almost carry him up and down. I was terrified he might slide too far if I wasn't there and get seriously hurt. It was time.

I asked Jan Spiers, a dog whisperer, to talk with him to be sure he was alright with the decision. She said he was close to the end and to be allowed to die now was acceptable. He did not want his life prolonged artificially and besides, she said, in his sleep, he had already met a white dog and together they ran up and down a lovely green field. We talked about who should be with him besides me and Steele. The other dogs were goofy, said Mr. Woodstock to Jan, so he didn't mind if they went off to play.

It was a long, hard weekend knowing the end was near. Dr. Foster and David came on Tuesday the 28th of March in their mobile clinic. Mr. Woodstock wanted to meet the doctor in a calm environment and lie down with me stroking his tummy. While Steele held his head, the vet placed the needle into his vein and he simply drifted into sleep and then quietly beyond.

We have buried my sweet fellow on the property. He has flower bushes planted over his grave and a three dog statue howling up to the heavens that we had bought in Mexico. On the front of his stone marker is an angel keeping guard. Although the dogs did not choose to witness his passing (as he had predicted they would not), we noticed that several hours after we buried him, they were lying down on the grass next to Mr. Woodstock's grave.

I have cried. My husband has cried. My daughter came with a flower bush and cried. My grand daughter called because she cared. My son emailed me twice because he loved him too. I hope my Virginia Gentlepup is happy. I shall never forget my man, Mr. Woodstock, my shadow, my companion, my love.

Dogs are our link to Paradise.
They don't know evil or jealousy
Or discontent.
To sit with a dog on a hillside
On a glorious afternoon
Is to be back in Eden,
Where doing nothing was not boring.
It was peace.
MILAN KUNDERA

The following story was written in the early '30s by my late father, Daly Highleyman. Most of the writing we found was completed well before my birth. This is but a small sample of his work which was bountiful. I dedicate this reprinting of Jerry Too to the memory of this multi-talented man about whom I really know so little.

JERRY TOO
Daly Highleyman

"Well," the old man said slowly, "if you want a story about a dog, I'll have to tell you about Jerry Too. Ever hear of him?"

"No, I haven't." I replied eagerly, "But I'd like to."

Funny thing, it does not start with the dog, Jerry Too, but with Jerry the lad who owned him. The first time that I saw Jerry, he was just a cracker kid who was crazy about dogs and used to hang around Miami's first track out at Hialeah. There is no dog track out there now but there was then. Nobody minded Jerry being around as he was a very useful youngster, always ready to do any little, odd job you asked him, never got in the way, and, besides, the dogs seemed to take to him naturally. Lord, how he loved being with the hounds!

Jerry never had any real job, at least, none officially at the track. Most kids at his age would just be a pest,

60   Patricia Daly-Lipe

always in the way, making a general nuisance of themselves. But not Jerry. He'd pitch right in and really go to work. He would pick up a bit of change here and there, if anyone happened to give it to him, but he would never ask for a dime for anything. That wasn't the way he was made, not by a long shot. If you would ask him to do something for you, he would do it for the love of being around the dogs and then, if you wanted to give him something afterwards that was alright with him but if you didn't—well, that was OK too. He just liked being there helping to train them, helping to exercise them, helping to feed them, helping to groom them, helping to do anything as long as it had to do with dogs.

Naturally, even in those days, Jerry wanted to be an owner. We all thought it was just a kid's idea that he'd get over—no one took him seriously. But it was sort of sad to hear him say, "Yes, sir, some day I'm going to have my own hound. Not just any old hound either, but a real sure 'nuff dog that's got good racing blood in him and can step out with the best of them, yes sir, step out with the best and win." He was so downright earnest about it that we would all coddle him along and tell him that he would have to work real hard so that he could buy that dog he kept talking about. No one made fun of his idea. He was much too serious about it and much too well liked for that. But at the same time, no one liked to tell him that greyhounds cost a lot of money, not only to buy but to keep and train as well. We all liked him, felt sorry for him, and made a pet of him. Everybody was his friend just as he was everybody's friend.

Each year that we went back to Miami, we expected to find that Jerry had grown up and out of his great love for dogs, had settled down to a steady job of some kind. It was just plain foolish the way that kid felt about the hounds, but it gave you a swell feeling to watch him with them just the same. That kid could do more with the dogs than any grown man in the place. Each year we would find him there waiting for us. He began to make a fair amount of money during the season even though he still held to that cockeyed idea of never asking for anything. Lord, Jerry could have named his own price, could have gotten a full job with any of the kennels by just taking his pick. But he was so good natured and willing to do anything for anyone that he seemed to prefer being more or less of a general mascot and handyman for the bunch. He did not want to work for just one of us but for all of us. So we pitched in and helped him out and shared him among us. We all felt generally responsible for seeing that he was kept busy. Don't think by that, that we looked upon Jerry as being a responsibility. Lord no! Just the opposite. We felt that he was common property and wished that he wasn't, at least if we were the one who finally got him. Each one of us expected that some day he would pick a favorite and stick to a steady job but he never did and when the new tracks began to spring up, he really was kept busy. You might ask him to do something for you and he would say, "Gosh, sir, Sadie Jane is running over at Biscayne tonight and I promised Mr. Cullen that I would go over with her." That is how busy we kept him but you could see that he hated to turn you down. There were no favorites with him. He liked us all and we just had to take our turn and that was that.

This sort of arrangement went on for several years and then came the great day when a bitch of Joe Martin's had a litter of pups. There had been other litters but this one seemed to be just a bit different. Perhaps it was because Jerry happened to be there when they were born, perhaps—I don't know. But that litter had a special spot in Jerry's heart, at least one of them did. We found that out later. He would go over to see those pups every day and there were even times that he would turn down a job because, as he would explain apologetically, he hadn't been over to see how Mr. Martin's pups were getting along. It turned out that there was one particular pup in that litter that took to Jerry the minute it opened its eyes. That little shaver knew from the start and would actually crawl out of the bunch to get to him before it was able to walk. That pup was a little beauty too. You can tell a good hound the minute it is born and Jerry—well, he was just plain nuts about that dog.

It became nosed about that Jerry had finally found a dog that he thought more of than all the other dogs put together. Of course, all dogs were still all aces to him but that pup had something that put it in a world all by himself. There was no doubt about it, Jerry worshipped the little begger. We all watched from the sidelines for a while and then one day, they selected me to go over and have a talk with Joe Martin.

"You know," Joe said the moment I came in, "That damn pup of Jerry's is the pick of the litter. I swear I don't know what to do!"

"What do you mean?" I asked uneasily, knowing what he meant just as well as he did. That's what I'd come to see him about because we all wanted to be in on it.

"Well—I hate to give up that pup—but you know how Jerry's always been about owning a dog, a real hound all of his own. Those two sort of belong to each other." Joe looked at me for a moment, then added, "Come on, I'll show you what I mean. Jerry's down there now."

There is no way to explain it but those two did belong to each other. The way that dog was making over Jerry you could tell that it had just been waiting all day long for him to come around and see it. Those two were all that mattered; neither one of them knew that we were standing there watching and if they had, it wouldn't have made any difference to them. They were so happy it sort of brought a catch in your throat. I looked at Joe and Joe looked at me and neither one said anything for a while, just stood there watching the kid and the pup playing together and feeling unnecessary.

"Jerry," Joe finally said rather hoarsely, "What do you think of that pup?"

"Oh, he's swell, Mr. Martin!" Jerry replied and his eyes were dancing, "He's going to be the best dog that ever chased a stuffed rabbit. Gosh, you just wait and see! He's all racer."

"Yes, Jerry, he's all racer. He's what you might call a real sure 'nuff dog." Joe and I just stood there a couple of lumps while the pup kept worrying Jerry's trouser leg until he finally picked it up.

"You know, Mr. Martin," Jerry began rather shyly, "I kind of wish you would do me a favor."

It gave me a start to hear him say that. I knew that he was crazy to have that dog but I never thought he would ask for it. It was so unlike Jerry, the Jerry I had known, the Jerry who never had asked for anything. I guess that both Joe and I were stunned—at least, neither of us said anything.

"I hate to ask it," Jerry hesitated and then continued with an effort, "But would you mind naming the pup Jerry, too?"

That completely broke me down and I could see that it hit Joe the same way. Eating his heart out for the dog and all he asked for was to name it. We both gulped a few times and Joe kept looking down at the ground and drew a line with his shoe.

"Yes, we'll name him Jerry Too. That's a good name. You see," he looked up at Jerry then down at the floor again, "I'm going to have him registered today and that's what I wanted to ask you, what name you wanted him to have." Joe seemed to clear his throat, "You see, Jerry, the pup is yours."

"The pup is what?" Jerry asked in a dazed manner, "The pup's what? I can't understand."

"Yours, d…it, it belongs to you! And see that you treat it right or I'll break your neck!" he added angrily, knowing full well that Jerry couldn't treat any dog any other way even if he tried. Funny how a man will act at times.

I didn't have anything I could say just then, so I took a run-out before I made a fool of myself, with Joe right behind me. As I left I caught a glimpse of Jerry standing there, hugging that pup and crying like a baby in spite of his twenty years.

The whole crowd of us were there when Jerry came in about an hour later to tell Joe that he couldn't take the pup, that he hadn't meant that or been hinting at it when he had spoken to him about the name. He had the pup with him to give back and everything. You could tell that it just about killed him to give that dog back but he felt that he had to, I guess. It meant so awfully much to him that he just couldn't keep it. It was too much pay for one man to give him for anything that he had done. It is queer how a kid like Jerry will argue against the one thing in the world he really wants more than anything else—but that is the way it was. He just couldn't keep him.

In the meantime, I'd explained to Joe the reason for my coming to see him that day, explaining how the rest of us felt, how the dog and Jerry seemed to belong to each other, and we wanted to chip in and make him a present of it. Lord love him, Joe had already made a gift of the dog to Jerry but when I'd gotten the crowd up there and he saw how anxious we all were to have a hand in on it, he let us chip in and make it a present from all of us. That is the reason we all were there when Jerry came in but even when he found out that it was a gift from the bunch of us, he still didn't think that he should keep the pup. Well, we stood our ground, coaxed and argued and lied, claiming that the transfer had already been made, until finally, we made him, forced him to keep the dog. I don't know who was happier, Jerry or the pup, for that dog knew just about as much about what was happening as any of us. The only difference was that pup didn't have any scruples about what was right or wrong. He just wanted to belong to Jerry and did not make any bones about it.

When Jerry walked out with that pup, you would have taken us for a lot of softies instead of hard boiled dog track men. We all developed colds and had places we had to go right away. But, believe me, we were a happy lot and very pleased with ourselves.

So Jerry became an owner and the way he raised and trained that dog was a joy to watch. He'd take him around with him on his odd jobs just to introduce him to the other dogs and tell him what fine racers they were. Of course that sounds as though Jerry spoiled and pampered the pup. Well, he did and he didn't. He would pet him and talk to him like a baby but Jerry Too soon realized that there was a job cut out for him and Jerry made him take his training very seriously. Jerry wasn't mean, he couldn't be, but he was very strict about his diet, his exercise and teaching him how to break out of a box. That wasn't play and yet that hound had such a natural love for the track that you couldn't call it work either.

He was crazy to race, it was born in him and you could tell that he was dying to get out there and run when he was all legs and paws. The minute he would see the other dogs on the track, he would get all excited and pull on that tiny leash of his and when the mechanical rabbit went whizzing by there just wasn't any way to keep him still. He would do everything but jump out of his skin. All greyhounds are born like that but some seem to have more of it than others. Jerry Too was one of those dogs.

Well, the season for the pup's first race finally came around. I know it seemed like an awfully long wait for Jerry and Jerry Too. It seemed pretty long for the rest of us for we were quite proud of that pup and you could tell from watching him work out that he was a winner. Of course he was Jerry's dog, there was no question about that, but I think that all of us had a sneaking sort of feeling that we were responsible, in a way, for his making a good showing. I know I had. He had it in him too; there was no question about that either. How that hound could run! He just ate up the track. Long, short, any and all distances were the same to him. When he put on speed, it really was speed! And when he got through, he was all set to keep on going, keep going as long as there was something to chase, fast and graceful as only a greyhound can be.

The night that Jerry Too ran, Jerry was all full of pride and emotion. The kid was walking on air. His dog was racing. I don't think he said a word before the race started. It was his night and he was too excited, too full of his dream coming true to say anything. He just came around to all of us in turn and showed us the program with Jerry Too listed in the first, himself as owner and trainer. Then he would point to the odds as though we didn't know that his hound was the favorite. Hell! we had all bet on him and we all expected to win. So had

Jerry. He had the stub sticking out of his pocket, just enough so you could see and know that Jerry Too wasn't going to run his first race without something on that soft, velvety nose of his.

Don't get the idea that this was any set-up race. It :wasn't. Jerry Too was against real class. Every hound in that race was fast, real fast. But Jerry Too was faster and he had that something that makes a dog or horse or man win, if you know what I mean.

Jerry was with the pup right up to the start of the race. Weighed him in, walked him around so that the spectators could look him over, muzzled him, took him out on the track past the judges' stand and paraded him before the grandstand. But Jerry Too didn't pay any attention to the crowd at all. He would just look up at Jerry lovingly, as though he were trying to tell him that he was going to win that race because—well—because they both wanted him to win. So did a lot of others want him to win but I doubt if either one of them ever gave it a thought. That race was theirs and the crowd that night was just something that happened along but didn't really count.

At last Jerry put him in the box with a final, affectionate pat on the head and the track was cleared. The only thing that you could hear was the dull, steely whirr of the rabbit picking up speed as it whirled around the track towards the starting point. Suddenly it slipped past the boxes at full speed, the lids flew back and the race was on.

God! Even now I hate to tell about that race. It was the most thrilling, the most spectacular race that I have ever seen and I hope I never see another one like it. Right at the start, Jerry Too was bumped coming out of the box. He and two other dogs went down in a heap and the other five went leaping on ahead.

I heard a sob and there, standing beside me, was Jerry. He had turned away and was crying. I put my arm around his shoulders and tried to comfort him. You could tell that his heart was breaking. He couldn't understand how or why such a thing could happen. It couldn't—not to his dog, not to Jerry Too—it just couldn't happen.

Just then I sensed a new note in the din around me. I looked back at the track. Jerry Too was up and streaking after the pack like a demon! How that dog ran! He showed even more speed than I though he had—and that was plenty. He had just caught the pack when I whirled Jerry around.

"Look! Jerry, you've got to look! Jerry Too is up! That's your dog, damn you! He's still in the race!" I shrieked at him.

Jerry grabbed my arm and howled. I don't know what he said but I do know that my arm was sore for days from the grip he had on it. I was doing some howling myself, everybody was. The place had gone mad. You don't get a thrill like that race more than once in a lifetime. They were at the turn now and Jerry Too had swung wide and was gliding along, slipping past first one dog and then another. Those hounds were going fast, mighty fast but Jerry Too seemed to skim over the track. He wasn't running, no hound could run that fast.

He was flying. His one idea was to get there and get there first!

Most hounds will try to head for the rail and force their way through the pack. But not Jerry Too. He had too much sense for that, he realized that it just couldn't be done, that he'd get boxed in, so he swung wide and around. Don't try to tell me that dogs can't think, don't have a brain. I've seen too many things that prove they can, at least, some of them can. Jerry Too really used his head when he took that wide swing. It brought him up into fourth place, mind you, at the beginning of the home stretch. Lord love him, that was good enough for a finish with the handicap that hound had started with. But it wasn't good enough for Jerry Too. He didn't know what it meant to give up. He flattened out and went after those three dogs ahead of him. What a finish that was!

I told you that those other hounds were fast, well, they were and they wanted to win, had the will to win and just burned up the track. But Jerry's pup was too much for them. He sort of eased past the dog ahead of him, caught the other two, and then those three dogs came flying down the track practically neck and neck. The rest of the pack dropped so far behind that they might just as well have quit. Even the fourth dog that Jerry Too had passed dropped way back. I guess that Jerry's pup had just taken the heart out of him. It was a three dog race from then on in and what a race! Jerry Too must have inspired those other two dogs. Neither one of them had run that fast before and neither one of them has run that fast since.

Down the stretch they came with every one yelling so loud that you couldn't hear yourself think. It was a stark, raving mad house. Who wouldn't go crazy watching a race like that? I realized that Jerry was beating the life out of me but I didn't seem to feel it. Jerry Too was the only thing that mattered. Jerry Too was in there to win even though it killed him.

Those three hounds were flying down the stretch, stride for stride, without a nose between them. Right at the finish, Jerry Too gave one last lunge forward that broke the tie. If he hadn't, no one would have known which dog won. But he gave the last lunge that carried him across the line first, crumpled, slid along in the dirt and the whole pack went over him.

He was dead when we got to him, dead as any dog can be. That last lunge may have done it, something had to give. But I swear that those dead eyes of his seemed to look up at Jerry as though they were trying to tell him something. The poor kid wasn't crying. It would have been better if he had been able to cry. But he couldn't. He just picked up Jerry Too and carried him into the little room at the track where they let him sleep, carried him in and laid him down on that shabby cot of his without saying a word and just sat there looking at him and stroking his dead head softly and lovingly. But he didn't utter a word.

I waited for the old man to go on, but he seemed to have finished.

"What happened to Jerry?" I asked finally. It sounded cold for me to ask it but I did not mean it that way.

"Happen to him? Why you've seen him often. He's the young fellow who is always with the dogs but never says a word. There he is over there," he said pointing to a young chap I had seen many times and taken for granted that he was born a mute. "He's been that way ever since. Always ready to do anything anyone asks him to do, just as he used to when he was a kid. But he never speaks."

"Can't you do anything for him?" I asked, "Why don't you try giving him another dog?"

The old man looked at me kindly and put his hand on my shoulder.

"Listen, young man," he replied, "We've tried that. We've tried everything. When we offered him another dog, he just looked at us in a puzzled way, shook his head and pointed to all the other dogs. Yes, I guess he feels that he had a one man dog, so now he's every dog's man."

SECTION II

ADVENTURES IN THE WORLD OF WATERS WILD

I love nature partly because she is not man, but a retreat from him. None of his institutions control or pervade her. Here is a different kind of right prevails. In her midst I can be glad with an entire gladness.

HENRY DAVID THOREAU

SAILING TRIP TO SINT MAARTEN FROM ANNAPOLIS, MARYLAND, NOVEMBER 1-13, 1996

Someday, after mastering the winds, the waves, the tides and gravity, we shall harness for God the energies of love, and then, for a second time in the history of the world, man will have discovered fire.

PIERRE TEILHARD DE CHARDIN, S.J.

Setting off always takes longer than you plan and, in the fall of 1996, it did. The fueling dock was out of order but we were assured that diesel would be available in two hours. Stuart, manager of Sun Sail, Annapolis, fetched our fuel while we topped off the water and ran through the check list: safety equipment, towel and sheet supply, cooking utensils, silverware, paper towels, sun block, and food.

Four individuals, Captain Clark, a forty year veteran of the high seas whom we always called (in due reverence and with affection), 'the Captain,' John, a pharmacist, Joe, John's brother, a botanist, and I, a female with some sailing experience, set out to deliver a forty foot Beneteau sailing sloop to the island of St. Maarten. Sun Sail, the company who owned the *Lodo del Mar* as she was named, wanted the boat in the Islands for their winter sailing school. The port of departure, Annapolis, loses most of its sailing population in the Fall despite its being the nicest, wind-wise, time of year to sail the Chesapeake Bay.

This new fiberglass, forty foot yacht has a nice and serviceable design. The cockpit is aft. Below deck, she has three staterooms, two aft and one forward, and two heads. The head in the bow has a sizable shower. The main cabin has been configured to accommodate several people at a time with the dining/reading/game/map table extending from mid-ships to the starboard side surrounded by a built-in semi-circular seat. The Captain's desk is at the foot of the steps leading up to the cockpit on the starboard side just in front of my berth and stateroom. On the port side of the main cabin is the galley with easy access for everyone to everything as it extends the entire length of the cabin.

After good-byes were said to loved ones and friends, the diesel fuel was topped off and the water supply was filled in both tanks, we finally set off at four

PM from Annapolis. Our destination, Sint Maarten, The West Indies, was some 1200 miles away. Or 1700 nautical miles according to our projected course. Our chosen route would bring us to and beyond Bermuda thus enabling us to take advantage of the 'westerlies' to the south of the British island. On a chart, this approach resembles an arc. A sailing ship making an ocean voyage is not concerned with making the shortest passage between two points, measured in miles. It is the weather, more particularly the wind which dictates the course. In some cases, pre-existing conditions like the Trade winds in the West Indies and the movement of the Gulf Stream flowing northwards and then eastwards can be counted on and used in charting the projected trip. The weather is another matter and, as much as we could foresee, was included in our calculations. With all these considerations, our estimated time at sea, beyond sight of land, was twelve days.

The wind was blowing at 15-18 knots so although we used the engine to leave the fueling dock, in no time we had the sails up and were quietly sailing down the Chesapeake Bay. The water lapped loudly against the sides of the *Lodo del Mar* as we cruised along at seven or eight knots pushed by a nice nor'eastern, just the right wind for going south.

We planned to sail all night and then stop at Cape Charles City. It is the last town on the Eastern Shore at the mouth of the Chesapeake Bay before entering the Atlantic Ocean. I was at the helm since this part of the voyage was quite safe and easy to handle. The sea was calm and the approaching night sky was clear. I was beginning to relish being back at sea. *And the lone seaman all the night/ Sails astonished among stars.* (Emerson) There is a wonderful feeling when all you can hear is the soft swish of the sea as it is invaded by the bow and the rippled sloshing of the water as it is left behind the stern. I turned on the navigation red and green running lights at the bow and the white light at the tip of the mast. The compass light came on automatically so I slipped the cover over its face to keep from being distracted from the impending darkness and the sea ahead.

The moon hasn't come up yet; the stars are brilliant. Pleiades, the jewel box of the sky, rides on the back of the bull, Taurus, while the mighty Sirius, the brightest star in the nighttime sky, glistens in the collar of the great dog, Canis major. In the middle is the belt of the hunter which is always on the celestial equator. This constellation is a sailor's guide. Beautiful Cumulus clouds with mare's tails are beginning to detail the night sky, an archetypal day on the Chesapeake Bay. The sun has left us completely now. It has become totally dark. After the sun and before the moon, the sky is black. I can't even see the sails to check for luffing. The light on the top of the mast has gone off so I can't see the wind indicator either. "Feel the wind on your face," the Captain instructs me. I am having trouble directing the craft. The wind is a bit volatile and weak. Not only the wind but the water presents problems. The tide is flowing against us to its rise at 10:30 PM. The warning bell goes off. We are in shallow water. The boat is going nowhere. We flip on the engine and a line from a crab pot shoots out behind the boat. I shut the motor and return to the sails.

All of a sudden there appeared to the port side, silhouetted behind the skyline of the Eastern Shore, a huge bright orange shape. It was eerily reminiscent of something from a Steven Spielberg movie; something totally surrealistic. I couldn't imagine what it might be nor who could have made such a structure. It was not like anything I had seen before in real life, nothing beyond the science fiction movies or children's fairy tales. Enormous and shiny, it was like a sculpture or some kind of modern art form. I was incredulous. The Captain roared with laughter and called the other crew members up from the cabin below where they were putting their belongings away. "That's the harvest moon!" Sure enough, as it rose up from the horizon and entered the night sky, the circle of light became smaller while losing some of its intense orange brilliance. Eventually the traditional white circle passed overhead.

"The gray mist on the sea's face, the gray dawn breaking...."

The great sea birds (Pelicans, Turns, Herons, Seagulls, and Cormorants) began their morning ritual as dawn approached. Bobbing and diving for fish, they were obviously enjoying a feeding frenzy. With a twenty-five year record for high temperatures, no rain and plenty of sunshine in Maryland, this was a lovely time to be on the Bay. Normally the nor'easterners which are heavy, cold and brutal, punctuate the Bay this time of year. We are so lucky.

As the morning approached with the reappearance of the sun, we acquired a porpoise escort. Actually, he may have been trying to warn us of the rising bay bottom. On a direct heading to Cape Charles City, there were shoals everywhere unmarked. Our draft was not that great (10 feet) but we began bumping into something and were forced to turn around. Before getting totally stuck, we adjusted the sails, captured the wind, heeled to the side changing the center of gravity to remove the keel from the sand bar. Slowly, with sails billowing in the wind, we slid away. Now in order to head north, we had to sail south and around to the port of Cape Charles. Going backward to go forward or forward to go backward is typical of sailing and takes some getting used to; it certainly defies all land-locked logic.

The channel was not well marked so we glided in slowly. We had plenty of time to observe and enjoy a convention of pelicans just a few yards off our starboard bow. The birds were gathered on an old wooden remnant of what looked like a fishing pier about one quarter mile away from the coast. Just behind the pelicans, we noticed heavy fingers of dense leaden Cirrocumulus clouds building up indicating foul weather. Cirrocumulus clouds are generally associated with fair weather, but when they thicken and lower, a storm is usually indicated. We needed to stock up quickly and scat to be in front of the impending rough weather.

Cape Charles City used to be a railroad headquarters. Before the Bay Bridge was built, railroad cars were loaded on barges in Norfolk and transported across the Bay to Cape Charles City to be reintroduced to tracks and continue their trip north. The barge ramp is still there but deserted and useless and the former dignity and grandeur of the little city, although it can still be found, appears to be ignored and in need of attention. We pulled along side the retaining wall and tied up. Cracks and holes corroded the site. Without the train trade, the government ignores the requests of the town and its vocal dock mistress, Mary Crockett, for financial assistance.

The town was just across a parking lot. The boat was safe...it was that kind of place...so we strolled over to the main street. There were few people around, but we did find one elderly man who looked like a resident. We asked where the best source of food in town could be found. He directed us to a restaurant around the corner. He was right; we had a sumptuous and very inexpensive lunch at Rebecca's Restaurant. This would be our last, level, sit-down meal before heading out to sea. The coleslaw, clam chowder, and bread pudding were particularly good: home cooking. Two ladies, Mrs. Frances Bender and her friend Bobbie, who were also having lunch offered to take me to a fish market just outside of town to stock up our rations. It wasn't far and I was happy to be in the company of such friendly women and interested in just what brought the two to this remote part of the world. Both were widows. Their husbands had come here years ago, worked, retired and died. Neither lady had the least idea about leaving the land that had become over the years, home.

The store was small but definitely not lacking in friendliness. Everyone there knew the ladies and all were delighted to share much enthusiasm for the local produce with me. At their suggestion, I purchased a basket of oysters ($15), a bag of little neck clams and a large Rockfish: all fresh and local.

> *If you would know the age of the earth, look upon the face of the sea in a storm.*

> JOSEPH CONRAD
> *The Mirror of the Sea*

Rolling seas, small chops, rain, gloom...three hours of continuous rolling offset by jerky movement and I was the first. Holding back as long as I could, I finally threw away my ladylike demeanor and let go over the side. Immediate relief but short lived. Soon everyone on board was heaving over the side, even (the last one, of course) the Captain. We had set sail as soon as I returned with my purchase of fish. The men already had raised the main and were holding the bow lines waiting for me to jump on board. Now, as we were jerked and tossed by severe seas, all I could think about was how nice it had been to walk on land!

From my sea stained journal:

"Rain, rain, cold and wet, the wind increases now (2 PM). We are really being tossed around. Forty miles to the Gulf Stream…southwest surge of the waves. 'They're humping up so we must be close the Gulf Stream,' said the Captain. 'The water will be sea-green. The seawater is always warmer than the rain.' That's our Captain, always the optimist. Had to reef the sails; more sail holds the boat better but can also tear. We are holding a heading of 120 degrees more or less. Rain continues; heavy wind. My face is splashed, first with fresh water from the sky then with salt water from the surf. We have reached the Gulf Stream. The cold wind of the north hits the warm Gulf Stream water which results in turbulence. Lightening. The pitching makes it very hard for me to hold the helm. Very scary in the dark. Very cold, wet from pitching surf and rain. My teeth are chattering; nausea comes back. Ten to twelve foot waves. Everyone is sick. The lovely Rockfish which our Captain had prepared with dried tomatoes had to be pitched."

I had a guest yesterday, actually two. The first was a Robin Redbreast. The winds were still blowing fiercely and must have pushed him off course. He was obviously lost. It was only a second before he left; instinct must have told him to leave. I am afraid he will become a meal for the sea birds. It is too far from land for the little fellow. The second visitor, a little brown bird, came back several times. At one point, he actually stood next to my feet. We fed him granola and bread crumbs, but like the Robin, he is too far from shore (approximately one hundred miles) and will probably not survive the elements.

> *Migration is not an easy or a pleasant thing for a tiny bird to face. It must turn deliberately from solid land, from food, shelter, a certain measure of security, and fly across an ocean unfriendly to its life, destitute of everything it needs. We make much of the heroism and endurance of our airmen and explorers. Perhaps one day we will rival the adventurous hope of the willow wren and chiff chaff, an ounce and a half of living courage, launching out with amazing confidence of prospect of storms, hardship, exhaustion, perhaps starvation and death…the tiny bird, before conditions force it—not driven by fear, but…drawn by Hope, commits itself with perfect confidence to that infinite ocean of air, where… all familiar landmarks will vanish, and if its strength fails it must be lost.*

> MARGARET CROPPER.
> *The House of Soul*

Sunday: "We have headed more south and east entailing a realignment of the sails. With a broad reach, we are making good time, eight or nine knots, but we are all still sick. Dramamine for everyone. It is a long, choppy night but a bit warmer. We watch as the clouds pass and all the stars come out, brilliant and clear. Saw a shooting star, a romantic name for debris from the solar system coming into our atmosphere and burning up."

Monday: "Sun at last! We watched it rise just to port of the mast. Beautiful day at sea. Our tummies are ready for food. To celebrate, our Captain prepared a pork roast with carrots, garlic, dried tomatoes and rice. Later, he is seen eating chocolate cheesecake with whipped cream! And only yesterday we were all sick! Had to use the engine to make up for lost time and lack of direction (need to sail south). Our 0600 position was 34° 42' N/ 68° 47' W. We are three hundred miles south and four hundred miles east of Annapolis. The water depth here is 4822 meters (about three miles)."

The proportions of a sailboat are important. The mast is generally one and a half times the length of the boat; the righting moment determines the size of sail. The keel counterbalances the sail. A 15-20 degree angle is usually best. Water is eight hundred times denser than air so a little bit of keel counter-balances a tall mast with full sail. The boat we are delivering is a Beneteau 40 with a roller reefing Genoa and a roller reefing main sail. The main is definitely too small for any serious racing. The boat is well balanced in heavy sea and inclement weather, but she is slow when the winds and sea are favorable. High speed appears to be eight knots. A spinnaker would have helped us in this voyage.

Sailing at night: Determine your angle from north by the compass then turn out all the lights. Locate a bright star and set (steer) your heading just as you would determine your course on a highway with reference to the center white line. Listen to the sails. This sound tells you the relative angle and the intensity of the wind. Changes in these sounds alert the helmsman/woman so that adjustments can be made to keep the boat on a proper heading. The setting of the sails may need to be adjusted or the heading may need to be changed to remain on the proper course.

At night, your eyes adjust and your hearing is keen. Large ships and freighters are always lit up and visible from great distances. They also are equipped with radar. As they approach or pass across the bow or stern, their movement and direction can be determined by the lights: green for starboard, red for port, amber for stern with the bow lights higher than stern as seen from the side. Trawlers have lights above the deck indicating their position and their situation (their nets and lines can trail hundreds of feet). Flashing lights indicate direction of a turn or backing down or with five short rapid blasts: danger.

There are several different ways of navigating. One based on the light intensity of the stars; a second, using a sextant and angles between the stars, Venus and Sirius; and a third with a modern GPS.

In order to determine a boat's position at sea, where no terrestrial points of reference exist, the stars become a friend of the sailor. The light intensity of stars and planets is measured by a magnitude scale of -30 to +25. This scale is inverted where our sun is a brightness of -27 and the faintest star that can be seen the most powerful telescope is around +25. This scale is not linear;

it is a mathematical scale based upon logarithms of 10. It has no upper and no lower limits (though the sun, in practice, sets one end). Every five numbers represent a one hundred times increase or decrease in brightness. The sun measures nearly -27; the sun-lit moon (the full moon) measures a magnitude of around -12.5. This means that the sun's light energy is not double the intensity of the moon but is one million times as bright as the moon. Venus has a magnitude of -4.4. You cannot see most stars and planets with the naked eye because they are too dim.

The historic method of calculation of a boat's position is to draw a triangle from your position to Venus then to Sirius (part of the constellation 'Big Dog,' always to the southeast of the constellation, Hunter) and back or to imagine a triangle from yourself to Venus, Sirius and back. Using the line from Venus to Sirius, draw a perpendicular line to determine the relationship of the sailboat to the stars. Where this perpendicular intersects the surface of the earth is the fix. A hand-held instrument called a sextant is used to measure the angle between this fixed line and the horizontal. By using this sextant angle and an accurate timepiece/clock/ chronometer, the sailor, after consulting appropriate tables and making extensive calculations, provided every step is done correctly, will be able to determine his position on the surface of the earth. This process is described by David Hays in *My Old Man and the Sea*:

> *Imagine the sun (moon, star) circling around the earth.*
> *Forgive me Copernicus, that's the way we do it. The sun*
> *is a round grape, the earth is an orange. Connect the*

*center of the grape and the center of the orange with a
taut line. The point where this line, the thread, pierces
the surface of the orange is called the GP, or geographical
position. This GP moves constantly as the sun or other
body goes around the earth. There is only one GP at any
second, and this exact point, for every second of every
day, is found from tables in an almanac you buy for
each year.*

On our boat, it is the Captain who makes all the
positioning calculations. The Captain uses a modern
radio-type instrument called GPS (Global Positioning
System). It establishes our exact position reinforcing
his sextant calculations using earth satellites instead of
stars. It can also be relied upon when a stellar fix can
not be established. The Magellan, a trade name for our
GPS uses the signals from four satellites to electronically
calculate a position. We are now 33° 13' north of the
equator and 67° 2' west of Greenwich, England (which
is 0° longitude).

Continuing in the journal:
"Election Day: I was woken up with the noise
of the engine being started and the throttle
being pushed way up. Water splashed through
the hatch; the boat heeled to its side. The crew
on watch has apparently lost control of their
direction/heading and, with a strong wind, the
boat is sailing full speed ahead but now under
power. Very unpleasant!
"We have drifted too far south and west. Must
now sail close-hauled with the engine."

Rolling out of my cot in the aft stateroom and, fumbling in the dark, I made my way into the main cabin. Contrary to the way the Captain sailed, these two men opted to turn on the compass light so that, looking up the steps from the cabin below to the cockpit above, I could see the faces of Joe and his brother illuminated. Their rain hoods had little or no effect on the water slapping at them from the stern and sides as the boat yawed in the throws of an angry sea. From above, the heavens were not kind, dumping a rushing torrent of rain and sleet on their faces. Shivering in their wet gear, they sat like gristly old men behind the big wheel, both using all their strength to hold the boat on course. It was a pathetic sight and it was a frightening sight. They were not smiling; instead, it was misery and despair that marked their expressions. This was not fun. To think, we had all volunteered for this job! In the dark of the cabin, I fumbled around trying to locate my foul weather gear. The boat was rocking and rolling in the heavy surf to the point that the only way to negotiate getting dressed was to hold on to the ceiling hand rail with one hand while somehow getting the pants on my legs and the jacket over my head. Then I had to find the safety harness. It could take up to twenty minutes to figure out all the straps and get them organized to go over the head, around the shoulders, crisscrossed around the waist and between the legs. The lifeline attaches to this harness. With lifeline in hand, I carefully negotiated the slippery steps to the deck above. This is a tricky maneuver in this kind of weather. We had all fallen at one time or another and I already had the bruises to prove it. There is no rhythm to this kind of rocking and rolling. With the rest of the crew, I attached my safety line to the stanchion and hung on for dear life until dawn when the weather changed. Incredibly, the Captain slept through it all!

> Morning: "The weather is lovely; the sun is shining. I can't believe last night's frightful situation ever happened but the scene still plays havoc in the 'palpitating vacuum of my memory' (George Millar's description of his perilous adventure in *A White Boat from England*). But that is the way of the sea! Three little porpoises are playing off our bow. They are exactly in sync with the pitch of the boat as they dive right in front and don't get hit. It is obviously a game for them. We watch them play for at least a half an hour."

Joe, who was manning the helm again after a brief sleep, told me more about the Magellan GPS. It is a great little instrument which was first used by the United States Government to protect the nation should an attack eliminate radar, etc. It is now in abundant circulation. There was a scare last year that the government would degrade the accuracy of the satellites' signals. They felt, however, that it was not necessary because the United States was not at war. There are at least thirteen satellites circling the globe but in order to achieve an accurate fix, direct contact with four is needed. GPS units, like our Magellan, can be used for hiking or visiting a foreign city as it always knows where you are and tracks the trail or route you take. The GPS unit we have on board is a Meridian XL Magellan GPS Satellite

Navigator. The brochure states: "The Global Positioning System (GPS) is operated by the US Government, which is solely responsible for the accuracy and maintenance of GPS." Further: "The accuracy of position fixes can be affected by the periodic adjustments to GPS satellites made by the US Government and is subject to change in accordance with the Department of Defense civil GPS user policy and Radio navigational Plan."

> Election Night: "Clinton won! We are thirty miles west of Bermuda. By six AM, we are circling the island. Since we arrived at the southern tip, we requested assistance in entering the harbor at Hamilton. The harbormaster would not allow us to enter from the south; rather, he required that we sail up the east side of the island, over the north end and down the shipping lanes to the Great Sound entrance in the south on the west side. A whole day lost! I took the helm at the north end of Bermuda, found the 'narrows' (indicated on the chart), an ocean lane marked with buoys, took the boat far west of the island to avoid reefs, and headed south with a compass reading of 130 degrees. A quarter of the way down, a rescue boat pulled up along side. We were, the man said, precariously close to the coral reefs and, to make matters worse, it was close to low tide. They had tried to reach us by VHF radio but we had all been on deck and hadn't heard. Furthermore, we were ordered back to customs in St. George despite the fact that we had registered with the dock master via VHF in Hamilton at three AM. New man; new rules. With heavy heart, we turned

the boat around again and retraced out steps to
the north, renewed our acquaintance with the
narrows, and entered the channel to St. George.
After six days at sea, we were so anxious to step
on terra firma."

St. George proved to be delightful and we
thoroughly enjoyed our brief stay (3 PM Wednesday
to 10 AM Thursday). Geographically, Bermuda is part
of the volcanic structures that have risen from the
mid-Atlantic rift (the spreading line that separates
the continents). The outer perimeter of the Bermuda
volcano is the coral reef area. The inside of the crater
or craters is filled with volcanic dust, limestone, and dirt
from Africa.

The sun was shining so we followed a path over the
top and down the west side of the island for a swim in a
protected pond of ocean water shielded from the sea by
monoliths of volcanic rocks. The water was 70 degrees.
Bermudians don't swim this time of year; in fact, their
season is quite short. On the climb back up the hill
after our swim, we noted the lush vegetation. A banana
tree growing alongside a picturesque pastel house
reminded me of southern California (where I grew up).
The banana "was probably introduced about 1616—the
first bunch of bananas displayed for sale in London,
England, came from Bermuda!" The book put out by
the Bermuda Department of Tourism further states
that "Banana leaves were once used to stuff mattresses."
Another fruit growing in Bermuda is the Paw Paw
(*Carica papaya*): "In old Bermuda, the juice of the green
fruit was used for ring worm and warts, now it is cooked

as a vegetable. When ripe, the fruit is yellow-orange."
Papaya juice contains a photolytic enzyme, Papain,
which digests the ringworm fungus. The only endemic
palm is the Bermuda Palmetto (*Sabal bermudiana*). Its
leaves were used by the early settlers to thatch their
roofs. They also made Bibby, "a very intoxicating drink"
from the sap. "In the 1700s, ladies' hats of Palmetto
leaves were the height of fashion in London." Another
native tree is the Olivewood Bark (*Assine laneana*), an
evergreen with leathery, dark-green leaves, yellowish-
white flowers (from late winter to early spring). It grows
slowly but lives to a great old age. We saw it growing on
the rocky hillsides.

A species of Juniper, the Burmuda Cedar (*Juniperus
bermudiana*) is another endemic tree. Its leaves are
scale-like, over-lapping one another with dark purple
berries. "The timber has been used for ship-building,
houses, furniture, and fuel. In the 1940s, scale insects
attacked these trees. By 1951, about 85% were dead,
many more were left in very poor state. Happily, a
reforestation programme has proved very successful."
From Madagascar comes the tall (up to 40 feet) Royal
Poinciana *(Delonix regia)* with its lovely regal red flowers
(late May to late September). The unofficial national
flower, however, is from the bermudiana (*Sisyrinchium
Bermudiana*). It is a "small herbaceous plant with leaves
5 to 8 inches long when fully grown. Narrow and knife-
shaped flowers have six purple petals that are yellow at
the base...." It only flowers mid-April to May."

As we strolled down the path toward the little town
of St. George, we saw oleander hedges with their pink

flowers and hibiscus with red flowers and bougainvillea growing over limestone walls and up the sides of dead trees with its glorious purple flowers. The bougainvillea is a native of Brazil. The oleander and hibiscus come from the tropical Pacific. They all thrive in this climate in the middle of the Atlantic Ocean.

Couldn't resist. We had to look for the famous Bermuda Onion. We found none. Apparently, the export trade ended in the 1930s because of import duty, competition from the United States and decreasing available land. The seed had been originally sent to Bermuda from England in 1616.

In the evening, we were enchanted with the musical chorus of the tree frogs (*Eleutherodactylus* j*ohnsonei and Eleutrerodactus gossei*). The small frog, Eleutherodactylus johnsonei, is only about one inch long and is more common. Both are brownish, nocturnal, and live in trees near the ground. They are very hard to spot. In the daytime, they hide under stones and leaf litter. Bermuda is home to the Giant Toad (*Bufo marinus*) as well. He is also called the 'road toad' because so many are killed on the road. These toads were brought over from Guyana in 1875 to control cockroaches and are now found in Hawaii and other Pacific rim islands.

To control the lizard population, the Kiskadee (*Pitangus sulphuratus)* was imported from Trinidad in 1957. It is "a large, flamboyant, yellow and brown typical fly-catcher…." However, instead of catching lizards, it preferred to fish on ponds and "catch insects in the air and eat berries, fruit, mice, and young birds—to the delight of our lizards!" (Bermuda Dept. of Tourism)

The perky little songbird we heard in the trees was the White-Eyed Vireo (Chick of the Village) or *Vireo guseus*. It sings year 'round and is a native of the island. Another native is the Bermuda Petrel or Cahow (*Preroclromia cahow*). This is a "famous endemic Bermuda seabird, believed extinct for nearly three hundred years until its rediscovery in 1951; it is one of the rarest birds in the world—under strict surveillance and protection of the Government. The Cahow lays a single egg each year and feeds at sea in the Gulf Stream." The Gulf Stream is four hundred miles west of Bermuda! The parents stay together to care for the one baby. If one parent dies, the other parent and the baby bird will die also because no food will be provided.

History abounds in Bermuda. Everyone seems to know some and embellish the rest. The Bermudians have triumphed financially from every major battle fought including battles between the British and the Americans. It even served as the port of origin for the blockade-runners (Confederate Naval forces). Pirates pillaged and plundered with permission from His or Her Majesty as long as the victims were not British ships. They were called "privateers." The loot was stored in Hamilton, the end of the island we never saw. Meanwhile, St. George wanted to establish itself as a city. To accomplish this status, a cathedral was begun but its construction came to a halt when another cathedral was quickly built in Hamilton. Nevertheless, St. Georgians are proud and supported the seat of power. The town hall, customs, cruise ship depot, shops galore, a golf club, excavations, a fortress, and beaches are all found at this end of the island.

There are one hundred and twenty-seven churches on the island supporting every religion that comes to its shores. School children wear uniforms and greet us with a very polite "good afternoon" as we walk the narrow streets. Above the 'pool' where we swam earlier were the remains of a fresh-water gathering station. Fresh water is a valuable commodity for sailors at sea. In our own case, after six days on the ocean, we needed ninety Imperial Gallons to re-top our water tanks.

We ended the evening with a gourmet dinner at The Carriage House, a treat from our 'crew.' The restaurant also houses a museum.

10 AM Thursday: "I'm at the helm. We're leaving the port of St. George passing the lovely old and new sailing vessels we had come to know with their tales of recent near-disasters at sea. We remember the men from Nova Scotia who passed the Berry Islands in a gale reaching Bermuda too rapidly at the expense of their craft, a wooden 34' sloop. They lost their dingy, hatches, windows, and almost lost their helmsman when a huge wave came up from behind and swept him overboard. His lifeline held; he went under the stern and came up when the craft righted herself. The man, in his fifties, did not look terribly fit anyway, a bit paunchy. The sea is a great force to be reckoned with: there is no compromising with her. I write this as we are again beyond the confines of St. George, beyond sight of the island and again ten to fifteen foot waves are pounding

at our port bow periodically drenching us in the cockpit. But the sun is out and the water is warm. Air temperature is 75 degrees.

"Night falls. No moon; we have to sail by ear and use the flashlight from time to time to check the compass. We must avoid the big punch from the high up north. We need to get east fast. We also want to be east of the southerlies which push west."

When you are on a train and uncomfortable as it sways back and forth on the track with a jerk here and there, you just sit back and resign yourself to the few hours of discomfort. On an airplane, when the turbulence necessitates fastening your seat belt and white knuckling for a few minutes, you know it will pass shortly. But when you are out at sea, the discomfort can last for days (as in days and nights non-stop). Inside, the cabin creaks; the dishes fall out as the cupboard door pops open; the coffee pot slips on the stove even though it is gimbaled and leaves coffee grinds all over the floor; hot bubbly water flows across the counter and down to join the grinds on the floor; hatches leak when the waves come crashing down; damp clothes hang everywhere in a futile attempt to dry them out; dishes and pots clang for attention in the sink; your feet slide and you are bumped and bruised; your body angle is 30 degrees or 130 degrees...all this is the joy of sailing in unrelenting high seas. The head (bathroom) is particularly challenging as your body is hurled forward at the door and lunged back to the sink. Outside, the helmsman develops biceps within hours and is lucky not to develop pneumonia as well. Actually, despite the cold and damp none of us has even a runny nose. Perhaps we have too much to do already just maintaining our balance. The Captain tells me we are in fresh, albeit damp, ocean air and bacteria and viruses can't find their way to us.

Last night a squall was spotted off to the north (a five-inch width to the eye). Time enough to recognize the need to reef the jib and main and to secure your lifeline close to where you will be needed the most. The most important detail is to predetermine the path you will take when the weather hits. We adjusted the sails to a broad reach and in anticipation of the storms up north we headed well to the east.

> "Things to see at night: Just after the sun drops into the horizon in the West, if you look east, you will see a gray crescent rising above that horizon. This gray crescent represents the curvature of the earth. It is actually the shadow cast by the planet herself.
>
> "Back down in the water that surrounds us, bioluminescence streaks out from the sides and the stern of the boat and over the tops of tufted waves. One minuscule agitated organism landed on my pant's leg and settled there for a second or two; he seemed almost friendly until he turned his light out. In the glow of the surf we saw what Joe described as 'round blobs of bioluminescent goo the size of a soft ball.' These Moon Nettles are a type of Jellyfish but they don't have stingers. They are amaphrodites and probably represent an early form of life. They have exoskeletons;

that is, the outer membrane holds the organism together. In the Chesapeake Bay, nettles were seen forty years ago that were fifteen feet long and red ("bloodsuckers"). Last month John, our other crew member, saw seven foot sea nettles at Solomon's Island. These organisms are part of nature's purification system he tells me. They eat plankton. (John is a Pharmacist) These Moon Nettles are part of this system as well. For supper, our Captain grilled mussels I had purchased in Cape Charles City. The barbecue is attached to the aft starboard rail. What a new and delectable taste!"

To measure the wind factor, we use the Beaufort Wind Scale. Admiral Francis Beaufort devised this scale in the nineteenth century. According to William Crawford, author of *Mariner's Weather,* those were the days of "wooden ships and iron men." It is a visual as opposed to digital measurement of wind speed and ranges from 0 to 17. A calm, smooth, mirror-like sea is of course '0,' smoke (the old fuel source being coal) rises vertically. The seventeen conditions are called "forces." Force 12 is a hurricane. Air fills with foam; the sea is completely white with driving spray; visibility greatly reduced. This condition is very rarely experienced on land; it is usually accompanied by widespread damage. I have never seen any higher than force 12 listed. Force 4 is described as "moderate breeze, small waves, becoming longer, fairly frequent white horses." With force 8, "foam is blown in well-defined streaks in the wind." Anxiety begins here.

We have been sailing almost consistently in force 7 to 8 on this trip but the final thrust has yet to hit us.

Generally speaking, most of the continental United States lies in a zone which has been called the prevailing westerly wind belt. Notice the word, 'prevailing.' It does not mean consistent but 'prevailing' does indicate the most frequent pattern of wind. In what are called the Horse latitudes, the prevailing winds are the northeast trades with a downward sweep to the east. This happens from approximately 30° N latitude down to the equator. The weather in the Horse latitudes is generally good although low clouds are common. The air that was heated in the tropics is usually cooled at higher altitudes and becomes less humid as it descends to the lower altitudes. Crossing this area in a sailboat can be difficult. Often days of stagnant air are followed by days of frenzied air activity and often can come unexpectedly. In the old days of sailing vessels carrying cargo to the New World, the cargo was often horses. With limited supplies of potable water available, it was a question of man or beast. As a result, many horses were thrown overboard, hence the name for this wind belt. The so-called doldrums separate the northeast trades from the southeast trades that have an upward sweep to the east. We have attempted to take advantage of all these factors in charting this course to St. Maarten.

> Saturday: "A quiet, slight breeze permits repair work to be done. The jib was torn at the foot during the tempestuous first days. We had rolled her back into the furling as far as the rip which naturally diminished our sail surface

(and, therefore, speed). Now was a good time to do some makeshift repair. In this light wind, we need as much sail surface as possible. Our Captain poked holes and wove a line through the sail; it is too heavy to sew. He then seized it in place. The main has seen her trials too. She has a tear mid-sail near the spreader. The Captain will tape this area.

"Joe brought up his fishing rod with a big spinner and lure. The line is now bobbing astern.

"We just found out that the Magellan GPS was still set on East-coast time. For several days we have been sailing in an easterly direction and have entered a new time zone. We assumed that the time change would automatically kick in. The sextant indicates that we are fifteen miles east of where the GPS put us.

"It is amazing what meals you can come up with using leftovers. Today's success: beaten eggs on turkey, carrots, onions, oil, and rice cooked in a closed pot and topped with cheese. Three hours later dessert was served: cooked fresh pears with yogurt."

Later this year, our Captain will be sailing around Cape Horn, from the Pacific to the Atlantic. He may be there on December 21st. On that day the sun will not set at Cape Horn. Here we already observe the declination of the sun as 16.5 degrees south. The sun's declination only goes 23.8 degrees south from the equator which is located along the Amazon. By the time we reach our destination, Sint Maarten, it will be 18 degrees.

Ptolemy was the first astronomer to measure the circumference of the earth. By knowing the circumference, the relative distance to the sun can be used in conjunction to compute location. Ptolemy took the measurement in the simplest fashion. He dug a well in the dessert. Then he measured the sun's shadow crossing over the well. That made a triangle. In ten months, this registered the movement of the sun in relation to the earth and thereby he was able to compute the exact size of the earth. It was too easy for most to believe.

In the fourteenth century, Copernicus was imprisoned for his accurate measurements of the globe. Every student of Euclidean geometry is acquainted with his theorems. In the fifteenth century, Galileo was incarcerated by the Holy Roman Church in order to squelch his findings; namely, that the earth rotates around the sun instead of the other way around. Although the prison cell was nice, he was impeded from validating his findings.

When the sun rises and sets, there is directly opposite (west or east) equally beautiful color. At sunrise and sunset, the sun's light travels tangentially to the earth's surface where you are. Because of the low level of the sun, its rays travel long distances through the lower and most dirty layers of our atmosphere. In so doing, the dust particles filter out much of the blue light and we see the remaining reddish colors from the color spectrum. When some clouds are present, the reddish glow is enhanced. On the boat with no interference from landmasses, it appears as if we are in the middle of this spectacle of light. It is because of this tangential factor that the light and colors appear on the opposite horizon. *"And the dawn comes up like thunder...."* (KIPLING)

> Saturday-Sunday night: "A long, breezeless night necessitated using the engine again. Time to identify the stars. Our four-hour night watch began at eight PM. After a four-hour rest, it will resume at four AM, my favorite watch since we are privy to the spectacular show of the morning sun."

To the port side (east) we look for Pleiades (the jewel box) with all its beautiful colors (greens, mauve, purples, and red) to rise above the horizon, then little dog (*Canis Minor*) with Procyon, the big star, the navigable star. Procyon, which means 'before the dog' because it rises before Sirius, the Dog Star, is the fifth nearest of the stars visible to the naked eye. By the time the belt of Orion reaches 0200 (30 degrees above the horizon), we can see the red light of the star Betelgeuse (originates from Arabic and means "armpit of the giant" according to Dennis L. Mammana, resident astronomer at the Reuben H. Fleet Space Theater in San Diego). Marking Orion's eastern shoulder, its angular width appears greater than the width of Mars. With a magnitude of +0.5, it is bright enough for its red color to be apparent to the naked eye. Hanging down from the belt of Orion is the sword of Orion. The middle "star" is not really a star. It is the Great Orion Nebula (M42), a quadruple star system in a cluster inside of which new stars and planetary systems are being born. It is nine billion miles

(1,500 light years) away. The hunter Orion's left knee is marked by one of the brightest stars in the sky: Rigel. Later in the evening sky, the mighty Sirius, the Dog Star, rises up. Between Sirius and Canis Minor we can see the Milky Way. Originally the name Canis Major referred only to Sirius. Sirius is twenty-five times brighter than our Sun but because of its distance, its magnitude is only -1.46; it is, nevertheless, the brightest star in the sky. Sirius appears to us as southeast of Orion. By four AM, I observe Venus making her debut. She has an incredible magnitude of -4.4, the brightest object out there except for the sun and the sun-lit moon. In the early morning, I use Venus to guide the boat.

With no wind, we took a break, turned into the source of the tiny breeze we had, pulled the jib over the bow, returned to a heading of 190 degrees or so and were at a halt. The water was most refreshing as we swam around, dove under to inspect the hull, and had some real cardiovascular activity.

Last night, unbeknownst to me, we passed through the Sargasso Sea. The Sargasso Sea is located between the West Indies and the Azores from about latitude 20° N to latitude 35° N. This is the area in the Atlantic Ocean where the currents swirl in a circle. This movement is the result of the prevailing surface currents around it, primarily the Gulf Stream. It is here in the Sargasso Sea that all the debris collects. The Sargasso is the center of the circle of movement. The debris comes from all over the Atlantic Ocean. At this time of year, the current movement, though always clockwise, is more and more

westerly as we proceed south. We had been warned in
Bermuda to be careful of ship wreckage in this area
from the recent hurricanes. Luckily we ran into nothing.

Four AM Watch: "The dawn breaks slowly. The
bright constellations grow dim. I'm steering by
the bright light of Venus two points ahead of the
beam on the port (east) side. We are not sailing.
The sails flap; the engine throbs softly. I look
west: no more stars. Light has pervaded the vista
of the universe. The light began as a pale blue
and yellow strip on the western horizon but as I
turn now, the horizon has become a spectacle:
orange, bright, bright orange lashes out violently,
clawing with its long, skinny, gnarled fingers any
clouds that might have been lazily dancing by. As I
stare in wonder, a tiny sparkle like a fourth of July
sparkler comes up, ever so small, peeping over
the horizon, waiting for just the right moment.
And when that moment comes, at the zenith of
brilliant orange, out pops the sun, whole, yellow,
and bright. The orange disappears and suddenly
it is daytime: more or less six AM as we creatures
here below call it."

Sunday noon: "We are at latitude 25° 50' N and
east of St. Maarten."

Monday morning: "Light diaphanous and pearly
fine with hairs and roots in the jet stream of the
upper atmosphere, the upper cirrus streak like
gauze while wisps of smoky gray dark brooding
cumulus are lurking on the horizon looking for
a chance to combine, each loaded with humidity.

The altocumulus looms to the west with its pearly tops puffing out from a pink background above, grey-blue to the horizon below. The water has a pink glow to the west; to the east it is a cerulean blue punctuated by short crests of Prussian blue. Foam gathers behind the boat as we move along at six or seven knots, still under power but with the assist of a little bit of wind. The clouds are important and should be included as weather 'instruments' on any boat. For example, the cumulus which we are looking at now needs vertical development above 10,000 feet before a thunder storm or squall can develop. We'll watch it closely."

In 1803, a gentleman named Mr. Luke Howard identified three basic cloud forms: cirrus, fiber-like strands extending in any direction; cumulus, flat-based heaps extending upward; and stratus, horizontal sheets widely spread out. But cloud nomenclature goes a step further. The aspect of altitude is considered and thus the names combine or are augmented with prefixes for clarity. 'Alto' really means high but as a prefix indicates a cloud formation in the middle altitude, 6500 to 20,000 feet. 'Cirro' means curl but when used as a prefix means the cloud is located in the high altitude zone, over 20,000 feet. 'Cirrus' is a complete name referring to a high cloud composed of ice crystals with a delicate, feathery appearance. 'Cumulo' or 'cumulus' come from the Latin meaning 'heap' and suggests a vertically developed pile. By itself, 'cumulus' represents a cloud structure: a dome rising from a flat base. 'Nimbo' or 'nimbus' refers to a cloud that is or will soon be raining.

'Strato' means 'spread out' but as a prefix refers to a cloud in the low part of the sky. 'Stratus' is a complete name that means a low-level spread of cloud which covers a large part of the sky. So there are two patterns: one that describes the appearance of the cloud and one that describes the altitude. The important thing for the sailor is to recognize the structures and to be able to anticipate what weather conditions might soon be keeping them company.

We are about 375 miles from St. Maarten and 600 miles from Bermuda, almost 1,500 miles from Annapolis. We are now crossing the most probable passage of Christopher Columbus. It is disputed where he actually made landfall first but it probably was Samana Cay, latitude 23° N. On this latitude we have seen two ships so far (we hadn't seen any other signs of civilization since we left Bermuda). One ship was a freighter probably headed for Africa/Gibraltar. The other was a cruise liner heading in the direction of Florida.

Getting back to Columbus: after his third trip to the new world, he was sent back in disgrace, chained and incarcerated for his decimation of the native population. He had initially encountered 250,000 or more people but, at the end of ten years, that population had been completely wiped out. Labor, mines, slaughter. Columbus was, in essence, Chief of State as well as Admiral of the Seas and as such had despotic control. What an awful blot on an ingenious sailor's character. He certainly knew his latitude, his prevailing winds; some days he was able to sail over 180 miles. As the

Captain says, "Columbus knew how to come off the wind." However, his flagship 'Santa Maria' was wrecked off the coast of what is now called Haiti and lost.

> *Who would separate waves from sea and say, 'These are waves but this is the sea.' Yet thoughts of waves forget thoughts of sea.*
> *Thoughts separate wholeness into parts and then forget wholeness. Waves and sea separate only in thoughts that have separated one thing from another and then have forgotten the separating.*
> *To return to the Tao, remember thoughtless wholeness.*

> *RAY GRIGG*
> *The Tao of Sailing*

The sky, the clouds, the surf, the sails, the invisible wind, the creatures of the sea, birds, and us...we are all connected. Never have I felt so much a part of and yet so humbled by nature as I do sitting by the wheel at night, alone with the stars and the sea, listening, listening.

> Monday: "The winds picked up around noon (remember the clouds?) and the ocean is rolling in undulating craters, waves at odds crashing into each other, foam tossed into the air, and our small craft traveling along sans motor at 6.5 plus knots. Finally!"
> Monday PM: "Blue sky, scattered clouds, warm temperature, and the ocean/sun/wind all to ourselves and lovely. Lunch consisted of everything we had little of and needed to finish: pine nuts, peanuts, onion, turkey, sweet peppers,

hot peppers, bell peppers, parsley, carrots, all served over brown rice. Fruit cake and pound cake with butterscotch sauce followed topped off with almond flavored herb tea. It is amazing what you can eat when you're out at sea! Still haven't caught a fish; the line is out and the barbecue is ready."

Monday night: "Twenty-five knot wind (Beaufort Scale, force 5) pulling west. The sky is hazy blocking the stars. It is a torn and ragged sea: lumpy. At the helm, I am surrounded with sound. The sea lapping or growling, the breeze passing through the shrouds with a chiming musical ring, a fog horn-like sound emanating from the Bimini frame, the shrill but soft wail of the EPIRB (electronic transponder indicating radio beacon). It is selective listening because the water which gurgles and the great sucking sound, the bobbling and whooshes are a comfort to a sailor's ears as he or she concentrates on the flow behind the boat. The intensity varies from Valkurian to romantic, a veritable orchestra, a symphony of sound. Then there are the not so sonorous sounds: the creaking and groaning of the bulkheads which must have come loose from the hull, the sound of the big three-bladed propeller hitting a high pitch as the boat accelerates off a wave. 'A parasitic drag posed by this encumbrance (the propeller) is a derisive to the sailing characteristic and abilities of this boat!' lamented the Captain. That and eight tons all up and a short rig and a roller reefing mainsail slowing us down. Very frustrating.

"We're seeing lots of flying fish. Some land on deck and if they are not found right away, die there. Their little bodies are about six inches long with black and white striped wings about four inches long. The total wingspan is about nine inches, enough to keep them airborne for flights sometimes up to three hundred feet."

We have to sail east of Anguilla Island and approach St. Maarten from the south. We should be there by dawn. We are now sailing over what is called the Puerto Rico Trench, over 8000 meters deep (about five miles). It is the deepest part of the Atlantic Ocean.

The sea below melds into the sky above. The sky above melds into the sea below. Only by remembered differences are sea and sky separate.

In the full middle, in both remembered sea and sky, is the sailboat, together with those together, united with those in union.

In the water of sea and the air of sky is the earth of ship and the fire of sailor, all together in a special togetherness.

Tao

Sint Maarten: 1200 miles south of Annapolis, 18° N latitude. We are almost there. But first we are raised out of our lethargy by one final burst of energy. It is our last challenge. Strong, gusty winds seemed to be coming from all directions at once. Similar to a squall, with gale force wind, it lasts but a few minutes. The Captain is called up for the emergency. The boat has jibed and the helmsman is terrified. The main sail is let out by undoing the traveler (the British call this the 'horse') and letting it slide out to beam reach and both sails are reefed. We jibe back into place; it is rough. The waves are in a frenzy. The wind is gyrating. Although I have attached my life line, I am still deathly afraid of being thrown or knocked overboard. The Captain, on the contrary, calmly makes the proper adjustments, puts the helmsman back on duty, and goes to bed! "No problem," he says.

The next day he tells me about the *Pride of Baltimore*. It was a similar situation that sunk the original *Pride of Baltimore*, a proud and noble tall ship, taking the life of one captain and two crew members. It happened just off the coast of Puerto Rico. The Captain called it a micro-burst. In this part of the world, micro-bursts and the horizontal winds they produce are common.

Micro bursts can be truly overpowering. It was just such a phenomenon which, in 1992, forced a jumbo jet into the ground just short of the Dallas airport runway. All passengers and crew were killed. Micro bursts cannot be predicted nor can they be avoided even with today's technology.

We arrive at dawn. The big cruise liners lie just outside the port waiting for the "proper time" to come in. Must please the customers after all! Meanwhile we sail right up to the dock, throw the lines, tie up and take our first tentative steps on terra firma. Five days later, I could still feel the swells rocking me.

STORY OF A CEMENT SCHOONER: THE TALISMAN

The sea never changes, and its works, for all the talk of men, are wrapped in mystery.

JOSEPH CONRAD

It began as a cry for help; I consented. It ended as a cry: my own. When I had first seen the ship, was I glad not to be considered as crew. Her sheer bulk, not just the length of 72 feet, but the weight, 60 tons, was intimidating enough. However, the source of her weight was more to the point. Made in South Africa perhaps as many as thirty years ago, she was fabricated out of cement. Not a veneer. A solid inch to two inches thick: cement inside, cement outside. Her paint was chipping; her lines were stiff. She would be departing just on the edge of winter, not promising weather. Very cold in a cement boat. Berthed at Solomon's Island, she had to traverse the Chesapeake Bay before entering the ocean. She then had a long, tedious trek taking her south around the tip of the Florida Keys and back up the Gulf of Mexico. Her destination: Biloxi, Mississippi.

For the voyage out of the Chesapeake, I was thankful not to be on board. As predicted, the weather was gruesome: cold and rainy. Near the Outer Banks, the *Talisman*, as she was named by the prior owner, encountered strong gales, icy rain, and powerful currents. A week later, I read that a beautiful old tall ship was lost in this very spot. Meanwhile, the cement schooner was slowly making her way south.

The call came from Charleston, South Carolina. "I have phoned everybody I can think of," said the Captain. "No one can make the trip. Please, we need your help." One of the crew, and there were only two besides the Captain, had broken his leg. The remaining man refused to go any further without a third person on board. I gave in; in part because I figured that they had arrived far enough south for warm weather. I was to stay with the boat only until she arrived at Fort Lauderdale, Florida. There, the new owner and his family would come aboard and take instructions from the Captain while sailing her around the keys and up to Biloxi.

It was exciting, I must admit, to be going out to sea again. It was especially pleasant to think of sailing off the coast of Florida with the warm breezes, the warm sea, and the friendly dolphins. I secured an immediate flight out of Charlottesville, Virginia, on USAir and arrived mid-afternoon expecting we would sail out right away. Not so.

The Captain and his first mate were at the airport to meet me. After gathering my duffel, we drove a rental car through the quaint and gracious streets of this southern belle of a city back to the boat. She was berthed at the very end of a series of attached docks off South Battery Street. It was here, just across the river, in 1862, that the first shot was fired by the Confederacy on Fort Sumter. Who could foresee then that some 646,392 lives would be lost and the South would be laid waste before this awful war ended.

I passed several people who had obviously made the long trek out the docks just to see her up close.

Commanding much attention from the press and curiosity seekers as well, she looked better than she had when I first viewed her in Maryland. Maybe it was just the notoriety she was getting.

Little tidbits of information were shared. Enough insight that, had I been smart, could have been put together to build a good scenario justifying getting the next flight back home. Instead, I was taken out to dinner then driven to the hospital to see the invalid. A huge cast ran from his foot to his hip. He must have been heavily sedated because he smiled a lot and appeared to be of excessively good cheer despite the fact he could not move. He would have to remain hospitalized several more days before attempting to fly home. His attitude was to be admired; it had been an ugly accident. The boat was heaving and battling giant waves and the weather channel had an alert out for all crafts. Matt, the young man, was attempting to remove the outboard motor from the back rail. The outboard belonged to a dinghy, which had already been lost overboard. Just in front of the back rail was the Mainsail traveler. Just as he was about to lift the motor, the boat surged up and crashed down again into the surf. Matt was completely thrown off balance and his foot was caught under the traveler. He heard it crack and knew immediately that the bone was broken. The Captain braced the leg with broken plastic battens from one of the sails. For two hours, he held the young man's leg as still as possible while waiting for the Coast Guard Emergency craft. Blood was streaming across the deck but the young man was tough. Meanwhile, the boat crashed up and down out of control, the surf pounding mercilessly until she hit a sand bar and was grounded. "His evacuation by Coast Guard rescue vessel left us hard up at falling tide," wrote the Captain in his log. "We've-floated the vessel on the incoming tide the following AM with the kindly help of a NW wind." Meanwhile, the wave action from the SW winds rolled and bobbed the boat. Green water splashed the decks and sprayed the cockpit for two hours at lowest tide.

Well before sailing any distance in the ocean, the Captain had cleaned the underside of the schooner. He had pulled monster barnacles off the propeller, rudder, hull, and transducer in the warmer waters of the Gulf Stream south of Cape Fear and had spent some time experimenting with the Furuno Depth Sounder. In the storm just outside Charleston, the Captain felt comfortable with the reliability of the craft in deep water and believed he had a dependable depth gauge. The *Talisman* grounded at a reading of thirty feet!

The surf pounded mercilessly as she sat on the sandy floor. She made the front page of the Charleston newspaper the next day. The news story centered on her being grounded. Not a mention was made of Matt's broken leg. I was there to take Matt's place but still we couldn't leave. More repairs were needed and the fuel tank had to be filled. To complete the latter task, we had to motor several miles up the river. There was only one fueling dock in the area that could accommodate a boat of this size. The weather was lovely, however, and I had an opportunity to acquaint myself with the ship before setting out to sea. Otherwise, half a day was wasted.

Finally, late afternoon, we set off. The water around Charleston had been calm; but even before we hit the ocean; I could see the swells. The weather report was not favorable either. Wind was coming from the south. This meant that we had to go to weather; the sails were useless. It is not pleasant to motor a sailboat. It was particularly unpleasant to motor *The Talisman*. Clearly, she was not built to go to weather. I was not nauseous; but, after only a few hours, my head was splitting. Her sixty tons were being beaten up by powerful surf. We stayed west of the Gulf Stream but just out of sight of land. The three of us rotated every four or five hours, taking our turn at the helm. Being at the helm of a seventy-two foot boat was a new experience for me. Talk about feeling power! It was an overwhelming responsibility. From the platform where the great wheel was, I looked down the long starboard side past the main cabin structure and the stay sail above and up to the bow with its second mast and sails. This was intimidating enough. However, to think that, at least for the four hours allotted to me, I was in charge of sixty tons of vessel...well, that is special. It was during my second shift that the cabin flooded.

Inside, the boat was quite impressive. The main cabin, or 'salon' as we called it, was huge. It had high ceilings, several built-in couches, a lovely wooden hand-carved dining table, a well-equipped galley, and plenty of open space. However, when I heard the commotion and looked down, this huge room was immersed in a surging wave. Water smashed against whichever side the boat heeled. The Captain was cursing the huge generator. Despite being new and expensive, it was not working.

That meant that the sump pump was not functioning. Like a chain gang, we had to bail out the water only to have more come in. The Captain finally located the source, a hole in the bow. While he patched up the hole from the inside as best he could, the other crewmember, Bob, had to bail out the water while I continued steering up top. Later that night, unbeknownst to me, while I was at the helm, the Captain, assisted by Bob, had hung over the bow attached by his lifeline with his head upside down and almost under water. While the boat pitched, he moved the giant anchor away from the hull. It had been the anchor that pierced the cement and caused the hole. This problem was fixed, but our troubles had only just begun.

Another day and I was at the helm again. It was late afternoon. We were progressing very slowly, maybe two or three knots. The big Ford motor was at full throttle but it had sixty tons to push through an unfriendly tide and oncoming wind. Suddenly, I heard a loud ripping noise, looked up to the bow, and saw the jib descend into the sea. Shreds of sail hung on the forward mast. It had split down the middle, probably because it was a very old, well-worn, and a poor quality sail to start with. The replacement sail was not much better. To be on the safe side, the Captain stitched up the more worn areas before putting up the backup sail. Until the wind direction changed, the sails were not doing much good anyway. Still, we wanted to be ready if and when the wind shift came.

The steering wheel was hydraulic. Periodically it would just spin and the boat would be on her own. The

Captain devised a plan. We placed a can of oil next to the wheel. When she stopped functioning, we opened the dome where the compass was located and poured the oil down the innards. This seemed to work…for the moment at least. We did have a backup: a twelve-foot long tiller up on the aft deck. Sure enough, it came to a point where we had to use the tiller. It was too powerful for me to hold alone so we arranged a pulley system. This way I had leverage and could control it reasonably well. Keep in mind, the tiller goes the opposite direction from the wheel. Going back and forth from the wheel to the tiller and back to the wheel again was a mental challenge. It demanded coordination and it took concentration, something difficult to do when confronted with possible panic, confusion, stress or a combination of all three.

We were moving so slowly that undoubtedly it would take more than a couple of days to get to Fort Lauderdale. The owner was notified and we decided to meet at a closer port since he was on a tight schedule and we had to accommodate him.

First we had to determine exactly where we were and then locate the nearest harbor. The boat was well equipped with radar, maps, and every kind of electronic communication I had ever seen, so this was one of the easier tasks. Our chosen destination was Fernandina Beach, Florida. Jacksonville was not that far away and the airport was even closer. Bob and I could fly home for Thanksgiving. The new owner and his family could take our places.

What our Captain remembered about this area and what we actually found were quite different. First we located the channel buoys, but our delight at finding them was short-lived. Despite following them carefully (red, right, returning), we could not locate a dock of any kind. It was well after dark and all we could see were fires from some big refineries. "This used to be a quiet little resort," the Captain said. I went below and called on the radio asking for some guidance from anyone listening. A friendly voice came on reporting that there was no dock master; the dock was closed for the winter. We could drop anchor or take our chances and pull up to the fuel dock. "When you see several small sailboats at anchor," the voice said, "you should see the dock." I thanked him. Little did he know how much we needed to go ashore, nor was he aware of our size and our condition. Everything below was wet, everything. It all had to be pulled up on the deck and aired out. Hopefully there would be sun the next day to dry it all out.

It took three tries, making large circles and negotiating the tide, but we did pull up to the very end of the fuel dock. Bob jumped off, grabbed the lines. I threw the big fenders over the side. The trip was over, at least for Bob and me. Or so I thought.

Once ashore, I went to investigate. A nice couple in a powerboat further up the dock told me about a bed and breakfast just up the road, easy walking distance. I found a telephone and called catching the night manager just before he closed. After hearing my tale of woe, he took pity and said he would wait up a little longer if we wished to take a couple of rooms for the night. I was delighted: a clean, dry bed and a good hot shower. We all slept well that night and enjoyed a scrumptious breakfast in the morning. The Florida Inn is one of the oldest Inns in the state. It is run by a couple from Connecticut who left the cold forever behind them. We were so lucky to have rooms for one night. Thanksgiving night they were full.

Thanksgiving morning we returned to the boat. Bob was ready to go to the airport. I was going to leave after the new owner arrived.

W.B. was a big man, not fat, just big, with broad shoulders and a muscular torso. I smiled to myself knowing that *The Talisman* would need his kind of strength. In his late forties, he seemed quite friendly in a provincial, unpretentious kind of way. He told us that he was a "Bible-carrying Christian" and that he had bought the boat because of the direction he felt the country was headed. He wanted a large seafaring vessel so that, if the country continued on the course it appeared to him to be on, he could load up his whole family and sail away. It sounded eccentric to me but it was his choice.

While he inspected the boat and chatted with the Captain, I went to the shower on shore to clean up and change for the flight home. When I reappeared, W.B. stopped me and requested what he called "a small favor." He had little sailing experience, he said, and his stepson, who would arrive shortly, had no sailing experience at all. "Could you please stay on just a few days more? Just until Fort Lauderdale?" His wife and his stepson's wife would join us there and I could leave. It was hard not to feel sorry for the man so I called my children and told them I would not be home for Thanksgiving dinner after all. Grabbing my newly packed duffel bag, I returned to the shower and changed back into sailing clothes. I was a deck hand once more. Satisfied, W.B. returned to the hotel where he had left his family the night before. They would all drive back later that afternoon so the wives could at least see the boat before the ladies headed south in their rented car to Fort Lauderdale. He and his stepson planned to learn from the Captain and me how to sail the schooner.

The Captain and I walked all over town looking for a restaurant to have Thanksgiving dinner. Everything was closed or, like the Florida Inn, was totally booked. So we settled for leftovers and took our goodies to the deck of *The Talisman*. Surrounded by cushions and sheets, towels and pillows, all airing out, we ate chicken and carrots and drank a glass of wine. This was our Thanksgiving feast. Actually, it was quite nice because the boat was quiet and the sun was shining. We folded all the sheets and towels and replaced all the cushions and rugs. Late in the afternoon, W.B. showed up with his wife, his stepson, and the stepson's wife. The wives were petite and dainty like little china dolls and fastidiously dressed. They could not hide their shock, even with the deck cleared. With no idea what to expect, obviously this ship did not meet even a remote expectation. The Captain and I decided right then that those two ladies would never sail this boat. I was not sure about the son either. W.B. was a big man but his stepson was small, skinny, and delicate looking. Quickly, good-byes were said, the ladies were kissed by their husbands and sent away; at least, I think they were sent away since they did not stay on the dock to see us off. The Captain put me at the helm, W.B. tossed the lines, and his son caught them, grabbed his stepfather's hand and was pulled on board. It was getting dark. The markers were easy to follow so I suggested that the new owner take the helm of his ship. He was nervous but clearly excited about his new toy…that is, until we hit the ocean.

W.B. had only sailed a couple of thirty-foot boats on the Great Lakes. He had never been out in the ocean. His stepson had never sailed at all. "Are the waves always this big?" he asked, fear coming through loud and clear. "No, they will settle down when the wind shifts," the Captain assured him. However, when the wind did shift, the sea still churned a bit. It is rarely glassy out at sea. W.B. was sick. His stepson was sicker. In fact, the young man was so sick I was frightened. Both popped seasick pills and went to bed.

That first night, the Captain and I took turns sailing throughout the night and into morning. The two invalids slept soundly. Exhausted, I was thrilled to see W.B. come up and ask if he could take the wheel. In a minute, I was asleep below. But not for long.

"There's water leaking. Come quickly!" yelled W.B. I grudgingly rolled out of my cot half expecting to see the tidal wave we had in the salon before. There was water but not nearly as much. Of course W.B. had not witnessed the prior performance. The Captain was already at work rigging up the hand pump he had purchased in Fernandina Beach along with hydraulic cement he had used to patch up the hole in the bow. The first place I looked was the former hole but it was completely dry. "Where is the water coming from this time?" I asked. "Just look at the depth here!" replied the Captain. The bilge was practically shallow, no more than a foot or two deep. No wonder the salon had high ceilings; we were standing down on the very bottom of the boat! Most boats have fairly deep bilge areas. On top of this, the automatic bilge pump was not working because the generator had a broken part and couldn't function without it. The Captain had instructed the wives to locate and purchase the part in Fort Lauderdale. At least that would straighten a few things out for the rest of the voyage.

Awkwardly, I carried the pump tubing up the steep steps to empty on the deck and over the side. That was another thing. The stairs were very steep: straight up and straight down. There was a metal pole, similar to a fireman's pole, to grab. Down the second step, you leaned forward and grabbed the pole. There was a braided rope at just that point on the pole. Obviously, many people had found the need to grab the pole over the years. When the boat was toiling through ocean waves, this braided rope was a real necessity for getting down below. Meanwhile, the hand pump worked reasonably well. The water had not risen too high but it had sloshed through the pantry door where the pots and pans were piled on the floor. They were filled with seawater. Water had also sloshed into the oven, which we never used, and the rugs were soaked. My feet were soaked also. This is not pleasant when it is cold. Despite being off the Florida coast, it was cold. It was especially cold down below in the cement-walled salon.

W.B. and his stepson continued to take the pills. This meant that they slept most of the time. When he was awake, however, W.B. was more than amenable to learn how to run the boat. His stepson, on the other hand, was ill as soon as he woke up. This was the pattern as we trudged along ever so slowly heading south. The winds continued to be unfavorable although they had come around a bit.

Again, it happened while I was at the helm. The engine was our main source of power, the sails adding very little momentum but enough to have them all up, including the Staysail. The engine began making a strange sound. I lowered the stick to slow it down but the noise continued. "Captain," I called. "There's something strange going on."

"Shut it off! Shut it off immediately!"

I did.

"Shut it off, I said!" growled the Captain.

"It is off!" I shouted back.

He ran down to the aft quarters where the stepson was sleeping and pulled up the floorboards.

"It's the drive shaft," he shouted.

As I peered down the back ladder, I could see oily water sloshing in the area he had uncovered. W.B. came to his assistance and I watched with disbelief as the Captain descended into the wet, oily hole. Blindly, because the shaft was below the flooring and there was no light, he groped and pulled and was able to disengage the broken part. He was soaked and filthy with black grease all over his hands and arms and oil on his clothes and in his hair. A nasty job. The next problem was finding a replacement or some facsimile of the part. Without the engine, our progress rate was reduced to a mere one to two knots. Fortunately, a replacement was found and back down the hole went the grubby Captain. After what seemed like a very long time, the word came up, "Turn on the engine!" Nothing. Back down the hole for an adjustment and out. "Try again!" Success! Back up to 4.6 knots. The stepson slept through the whole thing.

When at last he did come up, the stepson looked better. He took the helm for the first time. However, it was not more than two hours before he was heaving over the side. When I came up, W.B. was steering. "This wheel doesn't seem to be doing anything. Just spins 'round and 'round," he said. I rushed to read the coordinates. Fortunately, the sails had held us pretty true to course. I explained the oil routine. We took off the compass dome and poured. This time the wheel did not respond. The Captain, who was sacked out in utter exhaustion, had to be summoned. He instructed us to revert to the tiller. Even with the cable tied around for leverage, this was not fun. It was particularly unpleasant at night. The moon was on the wane so it was very dark on the upper deck.

The stepson kept trying to help but his nausea got the best of him. I was concerned. The third day out, I had a conversation—no, it was more like an argument—with the Captain. The night before, we had passed Cape Canaveral. By midmorning, it did not seem that we had progressed too far south of the Cape. We were close enough to the coast to judge by direct reckoning. While at the helm, I had watched as it took two hours to pass by a bridge on shore.

"How long will it take to reach the next port?" I asked.

It would be midnight at the soonest.

"How far are we from Cape Canaveral?"

"You mean going back?" He was incredulous.

"How long?" I repeated without hesitation.

It would take about six hours, maybe less, because the wind would be behind us.

"According to the weather channel," I said, "the wind will be coming from the north in twenty-four hours. Because of the boy's progressive illness, I think we should pull into the nearest port. Besides, there are so many things wrong with this boat." I pleaded and protested. He finally relented. It was true. The ship needed repair but not out at sea. In addition, despite the Captain's attempt to take the boy's mind off himself, the stepson was losing everything that went down. He was dehydrated and weak.

We came about. For the first time, wind filled the sails, adjustments were made for the new tack, and we were up to eight knots in no time. Soon we could turn the engine off and really sail. Before dark, we were back at the famous missile site. It was almost like coming home, just sailing into a proper seaport.

I was sure the stepson would leave. However, after being on land, taking a refreshing stroll, and eating a good dinner at a nearby restaurant, it was easier for his stepfather to convince him to stay onboard. Meanwhile, every half-hour, the two attempted to reach their wives by telephone. At ten PM, the message came through. The ladies had flown home. I knew it!

This was my departure point. I was sorry to leave Florida, but I was not sorry to see the last of *The Talisman.* No, that is not really true. I had learned so much not only about this unique boat but about myself. I could stay calm when a panic situation occurred. And I could handle the helm even when it became a huge tiller. I would never forget this journey and, in a funny way, I was grateful to have had the experience.

The Talisman never made it to Biloxi. She rounded the keys all right, the wind being on the right side, but she ran aground near Tallahassee. It was not a violent bump I was told. It was a soft landing, the depth finder still malfunctioning, but she cracked with the impact. The hull actually split on one side. The Captain admitted to me, after the fact, that he had his doubts as to the substructure. When he had repaired the hole in the bow, he had seen nothing in the way of a frame, no netting, no steel, nothing under the surface. Sure enough, the hull was only cement, no support. She must have been poured into a mold. Made in South Africa where there many have been few demands on her weather-wise, we supposed the cement had been more than adequate. Perhaps we were being overly sympathetic to the poor vessel.

When the sorry event happened, the stepson literally dove off the side and swam ashore. The father screamed, "My baby! My baby!" and dove after him. The Captain was left on the sinking ship. He threw the anchor to the side to tilt the boat away from the split as much as possible. Then he got on the radio. Harry of Tow Boat US Carabelle was summoned. He conferred with the Captain and said he would return the next morning. The Captain swam ashore to survey the wreck from the beach. People had gathered to gawk. Finally one lady came up and said, "Has anyone offered you a good meal?"

"No, Ma'am," replied the Captain. He hadn't eaten in two days.

"Why don't you come to our house? It is right up the beach. My husband and I would be happy to make you a little more comfortable. You could use a shower too," she said, not meaning to be unkind.

"Oh, yes ma'am." He was overwhelmed. There was no fresh water left on the boat. He was dirty and thirsty. The lady and her husband gave him a robe and, while he showered, washed his grubby clothes. He ate a scrumptious dinner, in the robe, and after dinner put on his clean clothes, ready to get back to work. "There are some nice people out there," he said when he recounted the tale to me later.

The next morning, Harry arrived with fifty pounds of hydraulic cement, another pump, battery, and a generator. It was twenty-one hours after the initial grounding. Together, they waded the stuff out to the boat. Working through the night and low tide, the Captain was able to repair and strengthen the hull. However, time was not on his side. The blessed northern wind that had produced the calm sea condition was posed to change the next day. *The Talisman*'s weakened hull could not have withstood a real shakeup. Harry agreed to attempt the re-float at high water that evening. He arrived at 13:30 and trenched, dug and pulled carefully so as not to exert undue pressure on the vessel. *The Talisman* came free at 24:00, fifty-three hours after her grounding, and was towed back to Carabelle docking at 04:00 Tuesday, December 10th.

The story ends here. The Captain was relieved of his command by the insurance company who took over. Oh, yes, the owner did show up, three days later. His stepson had rented a car and was already back home in Baton Rouge. W.B. was going home too. To some extent, he thanked the Captain but he was definitely shaken-up. We do not know how much he had paid for the boat nor how much he had her insured for, but she was declared a total loss. Most likely she has become part of an underwater seawall south of the tip of Florida.

SECTION III
THE EVOLUTIONARY JOURNEY: MAN AND NATURE

To see the world in a grain of sand,
And heaven in a wild flower,
Hold infinity in the palm of your hand,
And eternity in an hour.

WILLIAM BLAKE

Wandering and Wondering in the Redwood Forest of Northern California

The wonder is that we can see these trees and not wonder more.

RALPH WALDO EMERSON

From Big Sur to the Oregon border, Redwood forests and giant Sequoias grow all along Highway 101. We had driven up the coast specifically to see these ancient and inspiring trees. After finding a spot to park the car, we began our walk. Up close, we could see the scars left on some of the older trees. Nevertheless, they were still thriving. Later we learned that is because the bark of the Redwood tree is fireproof. (Redwoods can grow tissue to heal fire scarring, sometimes completely covering the scar.) The bark is also more than twelve inches thick and resists not only fires but insect attacks. The only thing these hardy trees are not immune from is people. With cars driving past and people walking around (like us), the soil is compacted and the short root system is imperiled. The Redwood trees can grow up to four hundred feet tall and get to be thirty feet thick. The difference between the Redwoods on the coast (*Sequoia sempervirens*) and those inland (*Sequoia gigantia*) is the trees near the coast are taller. Those located inland and on the mountain sides are thicker. The area we are exploring is part of the Redwood National and California State Park (RNSP) located on 112,512 acres near the coast in northern California.

In Humboldt Redwoods State Park, there is an area called Rockefeller Forest. This section of forest lies close beside Bull Creek and the Eel River, the last "wild" (no dam to block the flow) river in California. Here is one of the largest remaining tracts of contiguous uncut coastal redwood forest in the world. Within the park's 53,000 acres, there are more than 17,000 acres of old-growth forest. How do you define "old growth?" These trees are up to (and some exceeding) two thousand years old. In part, their longevity comes from the darkness caused by their thick tree growth which helps maintain moisture. The fallen trees also add nutrients for further growth.

When I was a child of eight or nine, my parents drove me up from arid southern California to visit these majestic trees. I have a photograph of our car driving across the length of a fallen tree and another picture showing the car being driven through a huge Sequoia. The drive-through tree is still there. Though devastated by fire on the inside, it is still alive. Park Rangers tell us this particular tree is purported to be some five thousand years old!

Although the Redwoods' root system is short, it is extremely strong. The trees also use their limbs for balance along with proximity to each other. The trees that do fall, however, do not decay for hundreds of years. Redwoods also have, interestingly enough, the smallest cones of any conifer yet they grow the highest and live the longest.

While in this lovely area, we learned a bit more about the animals who call this region home. The total Elk population had diminished to only fifteen when

President Theodore Roosevelt tried to rescue them from extinction. Indians had contributed to the problem with huge land fires as had settlers hunting for game. President Roosevelt failed because there was no territory for them to roam. Each elk needs one thousand, five hundred acres to roam. Not until the late 1940s were the elk granted designated protected areas. These were provided by the United States government.

After 1900, the Grizzly bear had no land either. In the early 19th century, the grizzly, or brown bears were found in most of California. Before the 1849 Gold Rush, Northern California or "Alta California" as it was called by the "Californios" from Mexico (both areas originally owned by Spain) was already a popular settlement. In 1846, the Sonoma settlers started a rebellion against Spain called the "Bear Flag Revolt." The settlers designed a banner with a star on a broad white stripe, inspired by the flag of the United States. They also added an image of the most powerful local creature they knew: the grizzly bear. Independence was quickly won and the grizzly bear was featured on a seal adopted in 1849. In 1953, the California grizzly became California's official state animal.

However, things weren't going so well for the grizzly himself. As we mentioned before, long before the Bear Flag Revolt, Indians, Spanish explorers and settlers were killing grizzly bears. Some adventurous cowboys even captured grizzlies using only horses and lariats. Although the grizzly bear population actually increased for awhile by preying on settlers' cattle for sustenance, their fate was sealed by humans. California was attracting more and more settlers. There was no respect for the bear. The Grizzly was being killed indiscriminately.

Whereas, California was once home to 10,000 grizzlies, by 1922 it became clear something had to be done to protect the bear population. Sadly, it was too late. Any surviving bears were too few to mate and carry on their kind. Despite their presence on the California state flag, the California grizzly had become extinct.

Although there has been a decline in spotted owl habitats, the species being listed as threatened in 1990, they have defied the odds. Contrary to the Grizzly, the spotted owls thrive in the redwoods, at least on managed timberlands within and around the ancient trees.

What we have learned to recognize is that nature is out there for us to admire and respect. It is there to teach us as well. Comparing my short life to an ancient tree that took root over two thousand years ago, how could I as a human expect to understand longevity? What I do understand is the human animal's ability to be so self-centered that his brain is functioning on an immediate gratification, impulsive mode. This behavior is short term. In the sixties, the expression was "If it feels good, do it!" Hopefully this self-serving generation won't ruin what came before and the next generations will be able to take the same walk through the Redwoods that we took.

When you enter a grove peopled with ancient trees, higher than the ordinary, and shutting out the sky with their thickly inter-twined branches, do not the stately shadows of the wood, the stillness of the place...then strike you with the presence of a deity?

SENECA

Dreams Affect the Waking Hours

To sleep: perchance to dream: ay, there's the rub;
For in that sleep of death, what dreams may come
When we have shuffled off this mortal coil....
                                    SHAKESPEARE (Hamlet)

Indeed, what dreams may come even before we have "shuffled off this mortal coil?" As a matter of fact, what is our life without a dream? What is this power a dream has over us even in our waking hours? Just what is a dream?

Dream translates as 'rêve' in French. Etymologically, this French word leads to another word, révéler, which means to reveal. 'Reveal' comes from the Latin 're' ('un') plus 'velare,' 'to cover,' also from 'velum' (veil) and thus translates to 'remove the veils.' Richard Strauss wrote an opera called *Der Frau Ohnen Schatten/The Woman Without a Shadow*. I saw it performed in San Francisco in the late seventies. The stage was literally veiled from the audience, but as the opera progressed, one veil at a time lifted and simultaneously, the plot revealed itself and played out more and more clearly before the eyes of the audience. Symbolism turned into reality.

The hero journey is inside of you; tear off the veils and open to the mystery of your SELF.

JOSEPH CAMPBELL

If we remove the veil or to use etymology again, 'fall back' ('re,' again, and 'velar,' to descend), we must fall back to something we already know or we will tumble endlessly into a chasm of darkness. To recover from the fall, we need support, some kind of reality.

Within each of us is a creative core that actively creates the universe.

ROBERT HAND

The reality within is as valid as the reality outside. The beauty of nature all around us can transport our thoughts, our wishes, our dreams to another level, an understanding beyond words, something truly beautiful. But disorder and chaos can also affect our dreams and our outlook. The following little essay was composed by my son when he was a young teenager in the early 1980s. It reflects his reaction even back then to what was and is still happening in the world around us.

LIFE AT THE TOP
Johnny Daly

I would like to introduce my self. My name is Albert Nosenbury. My friends call me Shnoz. I live in Alaska, in Nightsville. I work for the BFI, now the world's largest company.

The world is so heavily polluted with toxic waste and nuclear dispersal that one cannot go outside without a gas mask. Since the continental United States and Hawaii have been destroyed, Anchorage is now the Capital.

I wish mankind was not so selfish! I don't even know what a bird is. I would like to go back in time if I could.

I had a dream. That's why I am writing you this letter. I slipped on my polyfyboplastic suit and gas mask and took a walk. I leaned against a rock near Blackfish Pond. The water was a dark charcoal with an oily surface. The sky was a deep gray. The wind howled uncontrollably and the ground was stiff and rocky.

I fell asleep. I dreamed of a world like no other. The sky was blue and a yellow glare watered my eyes. Birds were singing, green strips rose above the ground with little, colorful platters. At a pond, there was water that was so incredibly clear that you could see weeds growing from the bottom. I saw an animal moving effortlessly through the water. I proceeded to sit under a tree with red things hanging from its branches. They were just like the things my grandfather told me about. He called them apples. I tried one and it tingled in my mouth but it was delicious. I ate more and more until I couldn't eat any more. Around me there were small animals eating and drinking out of the pond. This was high class. This was 'Life at the Top.' It became dark and a glow from the sky left me speechless. There was a cool breeze that filled my lungs and made me realize I had no gas mask on. A whistle roused me. It was pure music. Unfortunately, I woke up. My Utopia was a false act of conscious. Now my dream has retired to a nightmare. By the way, if you want to find my body, it is behind the nuclear waste canisters.

Here was a story conceived by a child in reaction over twenty years ago to what was happening in the world around him. When children can see the image so clearly, one wonders what happened to the adults who molded the world he perceives. A child has an advantage. He or she has no preconceptions, no prejudices. There is in a child a sense of marvel that propels him or her to question the familiar. The adult mind, on the contrary, is securely conditioned in culture, experience, pressures and what has been perceived as knowledge. The ordinary adult never bothers to consider questioning the familiar. However, "Curiosity has its own reason for existing," Einstein once explained. It is our hope this little tome has helped to open your adult mind to what is not found in texts, to accept what Einstein defines as the "mysterious."

The most beautiful experience we can have is the mysterious. It is the fundamental emotion that stands at the cradle of true art and true science. Whoever does not know it and can no longer wonder, no longer marvel, is as good as dead, and his eyes are dimmed.

ALBERT EINSTEIN

Let us remember, nature has her secrets; however, since we are part of nature, I believe she is willing to share if we are willing to throw away the rules, the preconceived ideas, the limitations we self-impose. Take the time to stand alone. Allow the silence to speak to you. Look, don't just see. Listen, don't simply hear. And when you are asleep, let the dreams enter. In the morning, try to remember where you went and what you saw in your dream. Wonder and marvel lest your eyes be dimmed.

TO SEE, USE YOUR HEART

A graduate of the Rudolf Steiner College wrote of his training in Waldorf education: "Rudolf Steiner College gave me the greatest gift of all.... That gift is the precious lesson of learning to see with the spirit what the eye cannot behold." Rudolf Steiner, a somewhat controversial Austrian-born philosopher opened a school in 1919 that defied the conventions of the day. The school and the method were named (ironically) after the Waldorf-Astoria cigarette factory in Stuttgard, Germany, where this first school was opened ostensibly for the employees' children. Today there are at least four hundred Waldorf schools in twenty-seven countries.

"I look into the world in which the sun is shining, in which the stars are sparkling, in which the stones repose. Where living plants are growing, where sentient beasts are living, where man, soul-gifted, gives the spirit a dwelling place. I look into the soul that lives within my being, the world-creator moves in sunlight and in soul-light, in wide world space without, in soul-depths within." (Recited by sophomores at the Sacramento Waldorf School as a pledge of spiritual alliance)

Steiner believed that education should focus on academic and artistic yet practical training. "Our highest endeavor must be to develop free human beings who are able of themselves to impart purpose and direction to their lives." (Rudolf Steiner) One of the key factors in the Waldorf approach to education is an appeal, especially during the early years before second grade, to imagination, touch, movement, and feeling. In fact, reading is not introduced until the end of first grade. "By not teaching reading, but instead giving them puppetry, stories, poems, verses, singing games, movement, and gesture, we're building a strong inner reservoir that children can later draw upon when they do learn to read." (Ann Pratt, founder of the Pine Hill Waldorf School in Wilton, NH). This "inner reservoir" is the core, the heart, intrinsic to learning but largely ignored by most schools and departments of education. The Waldorf schools emphasize what others do not: the fairy-tale magic of being a child. I would like to think that we never loose the wonder, excitement, magic, and spontaneity once we are adults. We are simply too busy to remember, to take the time to "see" what only the heart can know.

The etymology of the word 'courage' is 'coeur,' a French word meaning heart. And perhaps it does take courage in today's high-tech, fast-paced world, to stop and "see with the spirit what the eye cannot behold." I believe that exposure to the world's literary and artistic heritage, art appreciation in general, is more than an academic area of study; it is an exposure to our inheritance and a part of our very being. Education should, in my opinion, encompass not only the so-called rational mind; it needs to probe the instincts/the non-rational/the intuitive side of the brain/persona. We need to break out of the merely repetitive thought processes of our minds and open ourselves up to *receive* impulses which originate not in our thoughts, perhaps not even in our brain, but in another place where we find/feel the very source of creativity itself.

Most of our lives today are spent in non-creative activities. We organize our day; we work out things; we arrange/prepare/repeat/contrive this and that. But in that ten percent that is left, not even the whole ten percent is spent creating/inventing/changing existing patterns. Creativity is not a valued commodity today. I find this particularly upsetting.

"Children have the capacity to 'absorb' culture..." according to Maria Montessori (1870-1952). The first woman to become a physician in Italy, Maria Montessori did not initially dedicate herself to what was then considered a 'woman's job,' education. Specializing in psychiatry and pediatrics, she concentrated on scientific data as any man in her field would. In 1901, Montessori's focus changed. She was appointed Director of the new Orthophrenic School that was attached to the University of Rome. Formerly an asylum for "deficient and insane" children, it was an environment that stimulated her to do a meticulous study beginning with all the research previously done on the education of the mentally handicapped. Taking the scientific approach to education, Dr. Montessori pursued her work with objectivity basing her conclusions on observation and experimentation. Eventually she retired from the medical profession and dedicated herself to advocating the rights and intellectual potential of all children. "... education is not something which the teacher does, but it is a natural process which develops spontaneously in the human being," Dr. Montessori wrote about in a 'house for children' from *The Absorbent Mind*. The two key words to me in the work of Maria Montessori are: 'spontaneously' and 'absorbent.' Her research and the study of education in general is not just about children; it is the study of man as a whole, of his culture and his potential. Although Dr. Montessori was acknowledged as one of the world's leading educators, the implementation of her approach to learning has not been as widespread as one would hope. Only in recent years has her work been reevaluated and recognized by psychologists and developmental educators as not only insightful but clearly ahead of its time.

Many new theories of education are evolving today as we become aware of the significance of a holistic approach to learning. Knowles, Senge, Schmid, Lozanov, Gardner, Fuller, and Diamond are among the 'new' researchers in the development of so-called 'Accelerative Learning,' a method which is supposed to generate higher levels of thinking and creative problem solving. The term 'Accelerative Learning' was first introduced by Lozanov's followers in the United States in 1975.

Dr. Georgi Lozanov was a Bulgarian psychiatrist. In the 1960s, Dr. Lozanov was in fact the only psychotherapist in his country. In his late thirties, Dr.

Lovanov was already a famous man having cured patients from many strange psychic problems. He was also the leading parapsychologist. He believed that our psychic capacities surpassed everything we had achieved in our evolution as human beings. (I am reminded that it was Teilhard de Chardin who believed that the so-called Darwinian evolution of the species actually continues in the mind of man developing into what he, a Jesuit condemned by his own Church, called the *noosphere*. It is no wonder then that so many so-called 'new' theories are popping up all over the world proclaiming the same truisms about the human mind and its potential for learning and the great need for creativity research!) To return to Lozanov: in 1965, he went to India to study the psychic capacities of the Yogis. He found that some of the Yogis not only had unlimited capacity for memorizing data, but they also had an almost totally photographic memory. As a result of these findings, Dr. Lozanov developed a new form of learning. Putting his students in a comfortable environment, stretched out in comfy armchairs, he played music by Bach or Handel which he or another teacher recited entire phrases in a foreign language. The tone of the teacher's voice varied in synch with the rhythm of the music. The results of this new theory of learning were incredible. In two or three months, students were able to learn difficult languages like Chinese or Russian. No grammar is taught. Dr. Lozanov believes that our subconscious mind knows all the grammars of all the languages of the world. It is the fact that his students are placed in the *alpha* state that makes them receptive to the language. The alpha state is typically the state of our brain between sleeping and waking. The scientists tell us that it is in this state and only in this state that the two hemispheres of the brain are in harmony and "function in *mutual interdependency,* thus reaching the full potential of creative possibilities we dispose of." (Ch'i Genics Research) The learning process can almost be described as learning by absorption! The music acts as a kind of transmitter. In 1966, Dr. Lozanov first published the term, 'Suggestopedy," in Bulgarian and in 1967 in English at an international conference on psychosomatic medicine which was held in Rome. In 1976, Dr. Lozanov contributed to a contemporary accelerative method of learning (Suggestopaedia) but further scientific inquiry into the 'reserves of mind' led him to what he called 'Desuggestive Mental Training.'

Perhaps it is time to go back and look at Father Pierre Teilhard de Chardin's theories and philosophy. Teilhard de Chardin was born in 1881 in Auvergne, France, the son of a gentleman farmer whose interest in geology he came to share. When he was eighteen, he became a Jesuit and thirteen years later, he was ordained (1912). World War I broke out and the newly ordained priest chose to be a stretcher-bearer rather than a chaplain. He was awarded the Legion of Honour for his courage on the battle lines. In 1922 he graduated from the Sorbonne with a Ph.D. In 1923, Father Teilhard de Chardin traveled to China on his first paleontological and geologic mission. He participated in the discovery in 1929 of Peking man's skull, a clue to the so-called 'missing link.' His writing at this time reflects his desire to combine his fascination with paleontology and geology with his life's work as a theologian. He wrote about the evolutionary process viewing the universe and humanity as equal partners in that process, a kind of metaphysic of evolution. "Teilhard regarded basic trends in matter, gravitation, inertia, electromagnetism, and so on as being ordered toward the production of progressively more complex types of aggregate. This process led to the increasingly complex entities of atoms, molecules, cells, and organisms, until finally the human body evolved, with a nervous system sufficiently sophisticated to permit rational reflection, self-awareness, and moral responsibility. Teilhard argued that the appearance of man brought an additional dimension into the world. This he defines as the birth of reflection: animals know, but man knows that he knows...." He further states that the next step in the evolutionary process as it regards mankind is social. "The Age of Nations is past. The task before us now, if we would not perish, is to build the Earth." Anticipating James Lovelock's 'Gaia Hypothesis,' Teilhard de Chardin's writing reflects his concern for and respect of the earth as an autonomous personality. "We have reached a crossroads in human evolution where the only road which leads forward is toward a common passion.... To continue to place our hopes in a social order achieved by external violence would simply amount to our giving up all hope of carrying the Spirit of the Earth to its limits."

Most of his writing was condemned by the Church and he was forbidden to teach in his native France. He returned to China and worked for many years before being made the director of the Laboratory of Advanced Studies in Geology and Paleontology. However, the Second World War broke out and he was imprisoned

by the Japanese for six years. When he finally did
return to France in 1946, he was again forbidden to
publish any more of his philosophical work. He then
moved to the United States and worked at the Wenner-
Gren Foundation in New York City. It was under this
foundation's auspices that Teilhard de Chardin made
two paleontological and archeological expeditions to
South Africa. He died in New York in 1955 and is buried
next to the Hudson River, in the state of New York.

When his writings were published after his death,
they were met with both widespread interest and
controversy. I was a student at the Catholic University
of Louvain in Belgium in 1963-4 and remember the
University's stance against his work. Of course, since it
was forbidden, we all read whatever we could find!

Father Teilhard de Chardin "suggested that
the Earth in its evolutionary unfolding was growing
a new organ of consciousness, called the *noosphere*.
The *noosphere* is a 'planetary thinking network'—an
interlinked system of consciousness and information,
a global net of self-awareness, instantaneous feedback,
and planetary communication." (Judith Anodea)

> *We only have to look around us to see how complexity
> and psychic 'temperatures' are still rising: and rising no
> longer on the scale of the individual but now on that of
> the planet. This indication is so familiar to us that we
> cannot but recognize the objective, experiential, reality
> of a transformation of the planet 'as a whole.'*

PIERRE TEILHARD de CHARDIN, S.J.
The Heart of the Matter, 1950)

Antoine de St. Exupery, pilot and author of *The Little Prince (Le Petit Prince)* once shared his secret: "... It is only with the heart that one can see rightly; what is essential is invisible to the eye." And thus we return the pinnacle on which all these philosophies and movements depend: coeur (heart) = courage. "It is not our heads or our bodies which we must bring together, but our hearts...Humanity...is building its composite brain beneath our eyes. May it not be that tomorrow, through the logical and biological deepening of the movement drawing it together, it will find its *heart*, without which the ultimate wholeness of its power of unification can never be achieved?" (Teilhard de Chardin)

What Rudolf Steiner's instructors teach in the Waldorf schools: to learn "to see with the spirit what the eye cannot behold," where man, "the soul-bearer," "gives the spirit a place to dwell;" a school where the graduates believe in the orderliness of our universe, does this not reflect the philosophy of Teilhard de Chardin? And the modern movements in theories of education and the learning process, do they not reflect the sense of oneness, a convergence on the planet and with the planet anticipated by Teilhard de Chardin? And the spontaneity and 'absorption' of educational material which Maria Montessori considered 'natural' to all human beings, does this not reflect the present evolutionary stage of humanity? Further, does not the fact that we obviously can 'absorb' information as proven by Lozanov not convince us of the so-called other dimension, namely: the creative urge?

Progress is being made all over the world, the so-called progress named technology. But another avenue of progress is also being made all over the world and that is the progress of research in the field of creativity. It cannot be ignored that the creative endeavor has a spiritual side to it. Nor can it be said that the creative work results from technical know-how. Inspiration is a key factor and its roots may not be as nebulous as they first appear.

Genuine creative imagination does not just spring from the right hemisphere of the brain. I believe its roots come from a much deeper place: the heart.

> *What shall be my attitude toward other life? It can only be a piece with my attitude toward my own life. If I am a thinking being, I must regard other life than my own with equal reverence for I shall know that it longs for fullness and development as deeply as I do myself.*

> *Man can no longer live for himself alone. We must realize that all life is valuable and that we are united to all life. From this knowledge comes our spiritual relationship with the universe.*

ALBERT SCHWEITZER

SECTION IV
POETIC MEDITATIONS

I

On this earth there is oneness.
It is a rhythmic flow, a great symphony that is life.
Trees with roots, stems and leaves
Shells, fins, furs and wings, all living things.
Each has a purpose and to each, an end
And then...a new beginning.

Let us recapture the imagination of a child
See again the mystery, beauty and joy of God
Playing within and behind, beyond and above.
Unite with the intimacy of commitment.
Trust takes time
But the gift is there, waiting.

O taunt me not with anger and impatience.
Treat me not like the mushroom
Whom nature mocks with an umbrella,
Shielding her aspiring stem from the kiss of Apollo.

No, consider a small blade of grass
Growing on a rock in the woods,
So frail to have pushed through the hard
unyielding mass,
A miracle alone in the forest
Noticed because she's different,

So small in the grandeur of the tall trees.
Alone?...not really.

The sun caresses her blade; she bends back
for more.
And she grows,
Not to be tall like her neighbors,
But to be all she can be
Bending and straining,
Getting bigger and stronger.
A soft summer breeze soothes her, fondles her gently
And she responds, shyly,
Her small body trembles, sensitive, yielding.
The hardship of forcing her way through the rock
Left behind, forgotten.

Rains come and she drinks with greed the manna
of life.
"Grow, grow," she hears and again she responds.
The night comes.
The stars, gods of her universe, appear overhead.
"What am I to do?" she cries.
"Be, just be," they tell her.
She sleeps.

It is morning and the dew slips slowly down her
sides
As the sun comes back to encourage.
And so the days pass
Until one day she yields,
Yields to the earth and falls ever so gently,

Sliding off the rock down,
Down to the soft, sandy soil.

Do not be sad.
Her life was dear, her goal achieved.
She was what she was and she was meant to be.

II

On this earth, there is oneness.
A rhythmic flow, a great symphony that is life.
Trees with roots, stems and leaves
Shells, fins, furs and wings, all living things.
Each has a purpose and to each, an end
And then...a new beginning.

Let us recapture the imagination of a child
See once more the mystery, beauty and joy of God
Playing within and behind, beyond and above.
Unite with the intimacy of commitment.
Trust takes time
But the gift is there...waiting.

Anatta: The Key to Creativity
Sound and light,
Flashes from the dark
Penetrating the woods and streams within my shell
As I loose the wall, my body, and succumb to the rays
of light
And the rhythm of chords, shaking, quickening my
nerves
To loose oneself—myself—
To feel, to become,
To emerge, to grow and blend,

To breathe and be,
Without form, without parameters
Self-less.

Harmony
Subdued yet subjected to shades and shadows,
Soft, satiated, warm, plenty, pleased
Yet spilling over, gathering, collecting
Slithering across, melting onto and into
Not me but mine.

Calm, composed, yet piercing and passionate,
No corporal concept, only thoughts, feelings,
A pulse without rhythm, a movement without beat
Sometime lost, sometimes found, but through it all
Me and mine

The following poems were written by my late father,
Daly Highleyman, in the 1930s

Nature's Little Tree

Wave your branches, little tree
And spread your arms out wide
And let your leaves come trickling down
As breezes 'cross them slide

Stay patterned there against the sky
With tiny stars for light
And cast your shadows 'gainst the moon
Breathe deeply of the night

For you are nature, God's green tree
And though you stand alone
You're living, reaching toward the sky
Where other trees have grown

And all those stars you silhouette
Against a darkened sky
The rustling leaves that tumble down
The passing winds soft sigh

And all the green earth at your feet
The world and forest round
Where other trees in evening breeze
Do echo back your sound

They're all your friends and you're their life
So with each rising dawn
Just greet them with a leafy wave
Until your day has gone

Pan

I've seen the sun's rays streaking
Through the leaves of old trees creaking
And I've watched small wood nymphs peeping
From behind.

And I've listened to Pan playing
As I've watched the branches swaying
And I've heard what each was saying
Hoped to find.

For the trees wore bright green dresses
And the breeze brought soft caresses
Like the brush of silky tresses
'Gainst my cheek

While Pan's woodland flats did render
Music mad, yet full of splendor
That was cruel and yet so tender
Left me weak.

So I lay there quite enchanted
While close by his creatures panted
As they ran and danced and chanted
His mad song.

And I lay there almost dreaming;
While about all life was teeming
And within my hot blood steaming
Swept along.

Soon Pan's creatures 'came much bolder
An elf sat on my shoulder
And all youth seemed wiser, older
As he sang.

Though no words were in his singing,
Even now his rhythm ringing
Deep within, still leaves a stinging
Sort of pang.

For I know things best passed over
Or left buried 'neath the clover
Where no seeking eyes or rover
E'er will find

That the secret I was given
And for which the world has striven
Is a curse—when once it's given
And not kind.

Evening Shadows
A dusky sea before me lies
'Neath evening shadows—darkened skies
And slender palm trees gently nod
And find their rest and peace with God.

Patricia Daly-Lipe, Biography

Born in California, Patricia spent an equal amount of time living on the opposite coast in Washington, D.C., the home of several generations of her mother's family. When she was 18, her mother died of cancer. She returned to Vassar College (with a year at the Catholic University of Louvain, Belgium) earning a B.A. degree in Philosophy.

Later, as a single parent of three children, she and her young family raised and raced thoroughbred horses (winning at Santa Anita, Hollywood Park, Golden Gate Fields and Del Mar racetracks). She also rode in the hunter and jumper divisions at horse shows on both sides of the country.

After her children were grown, she completed a Masters degree followed by a Doctor of Philosophy in Humanities, specializing in Creative Arts and Communication. For several years, Dr. Daly taught English and writing to University students and adults, wrote for the *Evening Star* newspaper, *The Georgetowner* and *Uptowner newspapers* in Washington, D.C., *La Jolla Village News*, and Beach and Bay Press in San Diego, California. Her stories, poems, and articles have been published in magazines in seven states in the U.S., in the Caribbean, and across the seas in England.

Patricia now lives in Virginia with her husband (and first beau) Steele Lipe, M. D., three dogs, three horses (all rescues) and two cats and near her three children and six grandchildren. She is the author of five books. She also paints and as an artist she has had her work exhibited in galleries and juried shows. Two of her paintings appear as the cover of two of her books including 'Messages From Nature'. She was a past President of the National League of American Pen Women, La Jolla Branch as well as President of the DC Branch NLAPW. Recently, she was Historian for the DCDAC (Daughters of American Colonists). In 2002, Dr. Daly-Lipe's La Jolla book was the winner of the San Diego Book Awards Association. She was the recipient of the 2004 Woman of Achievement Award from the NLAPW, a Best Books Award Finalist, 1st runner up trophy winner of JADA Award Winning Novel Contest,. and, in 2007, Daly-Lipe was honored as a speaker for the National Capital District 36 Toastmasters Spring Conference. Her presentation was titled 'The Power of Words'. The Special Achievement Award was presented to Patricia Daly-Lipe for participation in the 2009 "'Golden Nib' Contest including an award of second place in poetry for 'A Poetic Meditation'. In 2010, Patricia was recognized as a VIP in the Cambridge Who's Who.

Please visit http://www.literarylady.com

Author on Hughey (Hugs & Kisses)

Made in the USA
Charleston, SC
07 January 2011